D1270042

Raoul held her gaze for longer than she felt comfortable with. He seemed to be seeing right through her façade.

It terrified her.

'You're scared,' Raoul pointed out wryly.

Lily raised her chin. 'Not of you.'

His gaze held hers in that quietly assessing way that unsettled her so much.

'I'm very glad to hear it. How could we ever work together if you're frightened of me?'

She blinked at him. 'You want to work with me?'

'Yes.'

'But I don't understand…'

'I quite like the idea of getting to know you, Lily Archer. I suspect no one else has achieved that before.'

She gave him a guarded look. 'I suppose you see me as yet another challenge to overcome?'

'No.' His eyes glanced briefly at her mouth before coming back to mesh with hers. 'I see you as a temptation I should resist.'

Her brows lifted. 'Should?'

'Can't,' he said, and before she could move even an inch out of his way he covered her mouth with his.

THOSE
SCANDALOUS CAFFARELLIS

Rich. Ruthless. Irresistible.

Brothers Rafe, Raoul and Remy
are better known as the Three Rs:

1. Rich—
Italy's most brilliant billionaires.

2. Ruthless—
they'll do anything to protect their place at the top.

3. Irresistible—
their business prowess is rivalled only by
their reputation in the bedroom.

(Just ask any glittering socialite they've ever met!)

Last month you read Rafe's story in:
NEVER SAY NO TO A CAFFARELLI
September 2013

This month read Raoul's story in:
NEVER UNDERESTIMATE A CAFFARELLI
October 2013

Next month read Remy's story in:
NEVER GAMBLE WITH A CAFFARELLI
November 2013

NEVER
UNDERESTIMATE
A CAFFARELLI

BY
MELANIE MILBURNE

First published in Great Britain 2013
by Mills & Boon, an imprint of Harlequin (UK) Limited.
Harlequin (UK) Limited, Eton House, 18-24 Paradise Road,
Richmond, Surrey TW9 1SR

© Melanie Milburne 2013

ISBN: 978 0 263 23557 9

Harlequin (UK) policy is to use papers that are natural, renewable and recyclable products and made from wood grown in sustainable forests. The logging and manufacturing process conform to the legal environmental regulations of the country of origin.

Printed and bound in Great Britain
by CPI Antony Rowe, Chippenham, Wiltshire

From as soon as **Melanie Milburne** could pick up a pen she knew she wanted to write. It was when she picked up her first Harlequin Mills and Boon at seventeen that she realised she wanted to write romance. After being distracted for a few years by meeting and marrying her own handsome hero, surgeon husband Steve, and having two boys, plus completing a Masters of Education and becoming a nationally ranked athlete (masters swimming), she decided to write. Five submissions later she sold her first book and is now a multi-published bestselling, award-winning *USA TODAY* author. In 2008 she won the Australian Romance Readers' Association most popular category/series romance, and in 2011 she won the prestigious Romance Writers of Australia R*BY award.

Melanie loves to hear from her readers via her website, www.melaniemilburne.com.au, or on Facebook: www.facebook.com/pages/Melanie-Milburne/351594482609

To Sharon Kendrick,
a Harlequin Mills & Boon sister and a dear friend. xxx

CHAPTER ONE

'BUT I NEVER work with male clients,' Lily said to her boss at the south London physical therapies rehabilitation clinic. 'You *know* that.'

'I know but this is such an amazing opportunity,' Valerie said. 'Raoul Caffarelli is from serious money. This four-week live-in post in Normandy will be worth a year's work to you. I can't send anyone else. Anyway, his brother absolutely insisted on you.'

Lily frowned. 'His brother?'

Valerie gave her eyes a little roll. 'Yes, well, apparently Raoul isn't too keen on working with anyone just now. He's become a bit reclusive since coming out of hospital. His older brother Rafe read about your work with Sheikh Kaseem Al-Balawi's daughter. He wants you to help his brother. He's willing to pay you very handsomely. I got the impression from him when he called that you could just about name your price.'

Lily chewed at her lower lip. The money was certainly attractive, especially given her mother's desperate circumstances right now, after yet another failed relationship had drained her bank account dry. But a live-in post with a man—even one currently confined to a wheelchair—was the stuff of her nightmares.

She hadn't been anywhere near a man in five years.

'I'm not doing it,' Lily said, turning to put another patient's file away. 'It's out of the question. You'll have to find someone else.'

'I don't think saying no is a going to be an option,' Valerie said. 'The Caffarelli brothers are known for their ruthless determination. Rafe wants Raoul to be his best man at his wedding in September. He believes you're the best person to get his brother back on his feet.'

Lily closed the drawer, turned and looked at her boss. 'What does he think I am, a miracle worker? His brother might never get back on his feet, let alone in a matter of weeks.'

'I know, but the least you could do is agree to work with him to see if it's possible,' Valerie said. 'It's a dream job— all expenses paid while you get to stay in a centuries-old château in rural Normandy. Do it, Lily. You'll be doing me a huge favour. It will really lift the profile of the clinic. This is exactly what we need right now to build on the work you did with the Sheikh's daughter. We'll be known as the holistic clinic for the rich and famous. Everyone will want to come here.'

Lily swallowed a tight knot of panic in her throat. Her heart was thumping such a rapid and jerky tattoo it felt as if she had just run up a skyscraper's flight of stairs. Her skin was clammy and her head felt as tight as if a vice were pressing against her temples. She tried to think of an escape route but each time she thought of one it was immediately roadblocked by her need to help her mother and her loyalty to her employer.

Could she do it?

'I'll need to see Mr Caffarelli's scans and reports from

his doctors. I might not be able to do much at all for him. It would be wrong to give him or his brother false hope.'

Valerie clicked the mouse at her computer. 'I have the scans and reports here. Rafe emailed them to me. I'll forward them to you.'

Lily looked at the reports a short time later in her office. Raoul Caffarelli had a spinal injury from a water-skiing accident. He had also sustained a badly broken right arm, although that was apparently healing. He had some feeling in his legs, but he was unable to stand upright without aid, and at this point in time he could not walk. The neurosurgical opinion was that he would be unlikely to regain full use of his legs, although they expected some minor improvement in his current mobility. But Lily had read similar reports before and tried not to let them influence her when dealing with a client.

Some spinal injuries could be devastatingly permanent, others relatively minor, and then there was everything in between. So much depended on the type of injury as well as a client's attitude and general state of health.

Lily liked to use a mix of therapies—the traditional things such as structured exercise, strength-training and massage, and some which were considered a little more on the alternative side, such as aromatherapy, dietary supplements and visualisation techniques.

The Sheikh's daughter, Halimah Al-Balawi, was one of her star clients. The young woman had been told by three neurosurgeons that she would never walk again. Lily had worked with her for three months; the improvement had been painstakingly slow at first, but finally Halimah had taken her first steps with the aid of parallel bars and she had continued to improve until she was able to walk unaided.

Lily sat back in her chair and chewed at a ragged end on her pinkie nail. For anyone else it would be a dream job to take on a man as rich and famous as Raoul Caffarelli. To spend a month in the lap of luxury working closely with a man every single woman on the planet would give ten years of her life to have one day or night with, let alone thirty-one of them. They would grab the opportunity with both hands and relish every minute of it.

But for her it would be a form of torture.

Her stomach recoiled at the thought of putting her hands on a hard male body. Working with a client as a physical therapist meant physical contact—*close* physical contact. Hands on flesh. Hands on muscles and tendons, stroking and massaging... *Touching.*

Her mobile rang from where it was sitting on her desk. She saw her mother's face come up on the screen and pressed the answer button. 'Hi, Mum. Are you OK?'

'Darling, I hate to bother you when you're at work, but the bank's been on the phone to me again. They're going to foreclose on the house if I don't come up with the last three months' mortgage payments. I tried to explain that it was Martin who siphoned off my account but they wouldn't listen.'

Lily felt her blood boil at how her mother had been scammed by a man she had met through an online dating service. Never a great judge of character at the best of times—although *she* was hardly one to talk, given what had happened to her on the night of her twenty-first birthday—her mother had foolishly trusted her new partner and was now paying heavily for it. That lowlife pond-scum had hacked into her mother's accounts and stolen her life savings.

Was fate twisting Lily's arm? How could she knock back this job when her mother was in such desperate need of financial support? Her mother had stalwartly stood by her during her lowest point. Those terrible dark days after her twenty-first birthday had almost sent her to the edge of sanity. But her mother had stood by her, putting her own life on hold to help Lily come out of that black hole of despair and self-loathing. Didn't she owe this to her mother?

It was only for a month.

Four weeks.

Thirty-one days.

It would feel like a lifetime.

'It's all right, Mum.' She took a scratchy little breath. 'I'm taking on a new client. It'll mean I'll be away in France for the whole of August but I'll ask them to pay me up-front. That will sort out the bank. You're not going to lose the house. Not if I can help it.'

Raoul scowled at his brother. 'I thought I told you I want to be left alone.'

Rafe blew out a breath of frustration. 'You can't spend the rest of your life holed up here like a recluse. What is wrong with you? Can't you see this is your best chance—maybe your only chance—of a recovery?'

Raoul wheeled his chair with his one good arm so he didn't have to face his brother. He knew Rafe meant well but the thought of having some young Englishwoman fussing over him with her snake-oil remedies was anathema to him right now. 'The best doctors in Italy said this is as good as it's going to get. I don't need to have this

Archer woman wasting my time and your money pretending it's going to be otherwise.'

'Look, I know you're still smarting about Clarissa
breaking off your engagement, but you can't hold it
against all women just because she—'

'This has *nothing* to do with Clarissa,' Raoul snapped
as he wheeled back round.

Rafe gave him a look that spoke volumes. 'You
weren't even in love with her. You just thought she ticked
all the boxes. The accident showed you her true colours.
The way I see it—and Poppy says the same—you had
a very lucky escape.'

Raoul's left hand gripped the chair so tightly he
thought his knuckles were going to explode through
his skin. 'You think I've been lucky? Look at me, Rafe.
I'm stuck in this chair! I can't even dress myself. Don't
insult me by saying I'm lucky.'

Rafe rubbed a hand over the top of his head. 'Sorry.
Bad choice of words.' He dropped his hand back by his
side. 'Will you at least meet her? Give her a trial run for
a week or even a couple of days? If it doesn't work out
then you can call it quits. You'll be the one in control of
whether she stays or goes.'

Raoul wheeled back over to the window to look at
the view over the fields where some of his most prized
thoroughbreds were grazing. He couldn't even go out
to them and stroke their velvet noses. He couldn't walk
over the soft springy grass. He was trapped in this chair,
trapped in his own body, in the body that for the last
thirty-four years had defined him as a person—as a *man*.
The doctors had told him he was luckier than most; he
still had feeling in his legs and full bladder and bowel

function. He supposedly still had sexual function, but what woman would want him now?

Hadn't Clarissa made that starkly clear?

He wanted his body back. He wanted his *life* back.

Who was to say this Archer woman was the miracle worker Rafe suggested? She could be the biggest charlatan out there. He didn't want to be taken for a ride, to be given false hopes only to have them dashed in the end. He was slowly coming to terms with his situation. He needed this time at the château to get his head around how life was going to be from now on. He wasn't ready to face the world just yet. The thought of the paparazzi tailing him to get the best pity shot made him sick to his stomach.

He just wanted to be left alone.

'One month, Raoul,' Rafe said into the silence. 'Please. Just give it a try.'

Raoul knew both of his brothers were worried about him. Remy, his younger brother, had been there the day before, doing his best to jolly him along like a male version of Pollyanna. His grandfather, Vittorio, had been less supportive, but Raoul had come to expect that from him. Vittorio was not the sort of man to offer sympathy or support. His speciality was to blame and to castigate.

'I'd like a week or two to think about it.'

There was a loaded silence.

Raoul turned his chair around again, suspicion crawling up his damaged spine like sticky spider's legs as he met his brother's sheepish dark brown gaze. 'You *haven't*.'

'She's waiting in the morning room,' Rafe said.

Raoul let out a string of colourful obscenities in French, Italian and English. Rage raced through his body like a fast-acting poison. He had never felt so powerless, so damned impotent, in his life. What did his brother think he was, a little child who couldn't make a sensible decision?

This was *his* sanctuary.

No one came here unless *he* invited them.

'Cool it,' Rafe said in an undertone. 'She'll hear you.'

'I don't care if she hears me! What the hell are you playing at?'

'I'm trying to help you, since you don't seem to want to help yourself,' Rafe said. 'I can't stand seeing you like this. Sitting around brooding, snapping everyone's head off if they so much as glance at you. You won't even go outside, for pity's sake. It's as if you've given up. You *can't* give up. You have to work through this.'

Raoul glared at his brother. 'I'll go outside when I can get out there under my own power. You had no right to bring that woman here without my permission. This is *my* house. Get her out of it.'

'She's staying,' Rafe said. 'I paid her up-front and I can't get a refund. It was part of her stipulation in accepting the post.'

Raoul flicked his eyes upwards in derision. 'Doesn't that tell you what sort of woman she is? For God's sake, Rafe, I thought you of all people would've had more sense. This is just a money grab. You wait and see— she'll walk out after a couple of days over something I said or did and do a happy dance all the way to the bank.'

'Miss Archer comes on very good recommendation,' Rafe said. 'She's highly trained and very experienced.'

Raoul gave a scoffing grunt. 'I just bet she is.'

'I'm going to leave you to get acquainted with her. I need to get back to Poppy; we have a wedding to organise. I want you there, Raoul, chair or no chair. Do you understand?'

Raoul let out a hiss. 'I'm not going to sit up there in front of everybody like some sort of freak show. Get Remy to be your best man.'

'You know what Remy is like. He'll fail to show up because something far more interesting has come across his radar. I want you to do it, and so does Poppy, and I don't want her disappointed.' Rafe moved to the door, holding it open as he added, 'I'll call you in a couple of weeks to see how you're doing. *Ciao.*'

Lily gripped her handbag on her lap with fingers that were ice cold in spite of the summer temperature. She'd heard shouting, and although she wasn't fluent in French or Italian she understood enough to know Raoul Caffarelli was not happy about her being here. Which was ironic, since she wasn't all that happy about being here, either. But with the money safely in her mother's mortgage account at least one worry had been shelved.

But her biggest worry lay ahead.

Being left alone in this huge old château with a man she had never met before was like something out of a horror movie. Her pulse was racing and her heart was hammering. She could feel the stickiness of perspiration between her shoulder blades and on her palms. The floor of her stomach was crawling with prickly feet of panic and she had to press her knees together to stop them from knocking against each other.

The morning-room door opened and Rafe Caffarelli came in with a grim look on his face. 'He's in the library. Try not to be put off by his surly attitude. Hopefully he'll improve a little on acquaintance. He's just frustrated and angry about his situation.'

Lily rose to her feet, still clutching her handbag like a shield. 'It's fine...' She moistened her paper-dry mouth. 'It must be very difficult for him....'

'It's a nightmare, for him and for me. I don't know how to reach him. He's locked everyone out.' He rubbed a hand over his face in a weary manner. 'He refuses to cooperate. I've never seen him like this. I knew he could be stubborn, but this is taking it to a whole new level.'

'It's still early days,' Lily said. 'Some people take months to accept what's happened to them. Others never accept it.'

'I want him at my wedding,' Rafe said with an implacable look. 'I don't care if we have to drag him or push him there kicking and screaming. I want him there.'

'I'll see what I can do,' Lily said. 'But I can't make any promises.'

'The housekeeper, Dominique, will assist you with anything you need,' he said. 'She will show you to your suite once you meet Raoul. There's a young guy called Sebastien who comes in each morning to help my brother shower and dress. Have you any questions?'

Hundreds, but they could wait. 'No, I think I've got it all under control.'

He gave her a brief nod and held the door open for her. 'I'll show you the way to the library but I think it's best if I leave you to it.' He twisted his mouth ruefully and added, 'I'm not my brother's favourite person right now.'

The library was on the same floor in the centuries-old château, but the sombre dark setting was in sharp contrast to the bright morning room where the sunlight had streamed in through a bank of windows that overlooked the rolling, verdant fields of the Normandy country-side. The library had only one window that let in lim-ited light, and there were three walls of floor-to-ceiling bookshelves that dominated the room, as well as a large leather-topped desk and an old-world globe positioned beside it. The smell of parchment and paper, leather and furniture polish gave Lily a sense of stepping back in time.

But her gaze was immediately drawn like a magnet to the silent figure seated in a wheelchair behind the desk. Raoul Caffarelli had the same breath-snatching good looks of his older brother, with glossy black hair, olive-toned skin and a rather stubborn, uncompromising-looking jaw. But his eyes were a green-flecked hazel instead of dark brown, and right now they were glittering at her in blis-tering anger.

'You'll forgive me for not rising.' His tone was clipped and unfriendly, his expression stony.

'I… Of course.'

'Unless you are hard of hearing or a complete and utter fool, you must realise by now I don't want you here.'

She lifted her chin, determined not to show him how intimidated she felt. 'I'm neither hard of hearing nor a fool.'

He measured her with his gaze for a long, pulsing moment. Lily could see his French-Italian heritage in his features and in his bearing. There was a hint of the proud aristocrat in him; it was there in the broad set of his shoulders and the way he held himself in spite of being confined to a chair. He was taller than average—she estimated two or three inches over six feet—and was obviously a man who had been intensely physically active prior to his accident. She could see the well-formed muscles of his chest and arms through the fine cotton of the shirt he was wearing. His right arm was still in a plaster cast but his hands looked strong and capable. His face was cleanly shaven but the shadow of regrowth was evident, suggesting potent male hormones. His nose was a little more Roman than his brother's, and there were lines about his mouth that gave him a slightly drawn look, as if he had lost weight recently. His mouth was set in an intractable line, flattened by his mood and temper, and she wondered what it would look like if he smiled.

Lily pulled back from her thoughts with a little start. She was not here to make him smile. She was here to see if she could make him walk, and the sooner she got on with the job, the sooner she could leave.

'I suppose my brother has given you all the gory details of my condition?' he said, still pinning her with that intimidating gaze.

'I've seen your scans and read the doctors' and physiotherapists' reports.'

A dark brow lifted above his left eye, almost accusingly. 'And?'

She rolled her lips together to moisten them, trying to ignore the annoying jackhammer beat of her heart. 'I think it's worth trying some of my methods. I've had some success with clients with similar injuries to yours.'

'So, what are some of your methods?' His top lip curled mockingly. 'Waving incense around? Chanting mantras? Reading auras? Laying on of hands?'

Lily felt a little spurt of anger shoot through her blood. She was used to people rubbishing her holistic approach but somehow his sarcastic tone got under her skin. But he would be laughing on the other side of his face if she got him back on his feet. The challenge to do so was suddenly rather more attractive than it had been before. 'I use a combination of traditional therapies and some complementary ones. It depends.'

'On what?'

'On the client. I take into consideration their diet and lifestyle, their sleeping habits, their mental state and—'

'Let me guess—you read their tarot cards or give them a zodiac reading.'

Lily pursed her mouth to stop herself from issuing a stinging riposte. He was quite possibly the rudest man she'd ever met. Arrogant, too, but she supposed that came from his privileged background. He was a spoilt, over-indulged playboy who had been handed everything on a silver platter. His surly, 'poor me' attitude was just typical of someone who'd never had to work for anything in his life. He had it so good compared to some of her clients. At least he had the money to set himself up. He had people to wait on him, to take care of him. He had a family who refused to give up on him. Didn't he realise that while he was in his luxury château feeling sorry for himself, there were people out in the world who were homeless or starving with no one to care what happened to them from one day to the next?

'I'm a Taurus, in case you're wondering,' he said.

She gave him an arch look. 'That explains the bull-headedness.'

'I can be very stubborn.' He gave her another measuring look. 'But I suspect you can, too.'

'I like to call it persistence,' Lily said. 'I don't believe in giving up on something until I've put in a decent effort.'

He drummed the fingers of his left hand on the arm-rest of his wheelchair, an almost absentminded move-ment that seemed overly loud in the silence.

Lily felt the slow, assessing sweep of his gaze again. Was he comparing her to all the women he had dated? If so, he would find her sadly lacking. She didn't dress to impress. She didn't wear make-up as a rule and she wore plain Jane clothes that hid her figure and her past.

'I'm not sure what to do with you.' He glared at her darkly. 'It's not like I can physically throw you out.'

Lily sent him a warning in her gaze. 'I can assure you, Monsieur Caffarelli, I would put up a spectacular fight if you laid even a single finger on me.'

One of his brows went up in an arc. 'Well, well, well; the seemingly demure Miss Archer has a sting in her tail. Scorpio?'

She ground her teeth. 'Virgo.'

'Detailed. Nit-picking. Pedantic.'

'I prefer to think of it as thorough.'

A ghost of a smile tilted the edge of his mouth. It to-tally transformed his features and Lily had to remind herself to breathe.

But the half smile was gone almost as soon as it had appeared. His expression darkened again and his gaze singed hers. 'I've had weeks of physical therapy, Miss Archer, and none of it has worked, as you can see. I can't see how you could succeed where others more qualified than you have failed.'

'It's still early days,' Lily said. 'The body can take months, if not years, to recover from trauma.'

Cynicism made his eyes glitter. 'You're not offering your services for years, though, are you, Miss Archer? My prediction is you'll last one or two days, three at the most, and then you'll be off with a nice fat little wad of cash in your bank account. I've met your type before— you exploit people who are desperate. You've got nothing to offer me and we both know it.'

'On the contrary, I think I can help you,' Lily said. 'You're at a critical stage in your recovery. You should be supervised while exercising—'

'Supervised?' He barked the word at her. 'I'm not a child who needs supervising while playing on the monkey bars.'

'I didn't say that. I just meant that you have to—'

'I will do it *my* way,' he said with indomitable force. 'I don't want your help. I didn't ask for it. And I didn't pay for it. I know what I have to do and I'm doing it, and I prefer to do it alone. Do us both a favour and catch the next flight back to London.'

Lily stared him down even though it took an enormous effort to hold that diamond-hard gaze. His anger was coming off him in waves that sent crackles of electricity through the air. She could even feel her skin tightening all over her body, as if those invisible currents were flowing over and through her. She could even feel her blood heating; it was pounding through her veins as if she had taken a shot of adrenalin. 'You do realise if I leave now your brother will lose a considerable amount of money? There's a no-refund clause in my contract.'

His mouth thinned in disdain. 'Let him lose it. It's no skin off my nose.'

Lily was shocked. Was he really prepared to forfeit an amount most people didn't even earn in a year? And it wasn't even his money. His assumption she would take the money and go made her all the more determined to stay. Her conscience wouldn't allow her to take the money for nothing. He would think she was an unscrupulous gold digger and, given how high profile the Caffarelli name was, it would quite possibly tarnish the reputation of the clinic if word got out that she'd left without doing a day's work.

Besides, she was a little intrigued by his resistance to rehabilitation. Didn't he want to improve his mobility, or had he simply given up? Some clients found it very hard to adjust to the smallest of limitations put on them, while others coped remarkably well in spite of far worse injuries.

He was in good physical health, which was always a bonus in hoping for a positive outcome in rehabilitation, but his state of mind suggested he had not yet come to terms with what had happened to him. He reminded her of an alpha wolf who had secluded himself away to lick his wounds while no one was watching.

But then, hadn't she done the very same thing five years ago?

Lily held his steely gaze. 'I have no way of getting to the airport now that your brother has left.'

'Then I'll get one of the stableboys to drive you.'

'I'm not leaving.'

A muscle worked in his jaw. 'I don't want you here.'

'You've made that more than obvious,' Lily said huffily. 'I didn't expect a red carpet to be rolled out or anything, but the least you could've done is be civil. Or does being filthy rich mean you can act like a total jerk and get away with it?'

His gaze warred with hers for a throbbing moment. 'My brother had no right to bring you here without my permission.'

'So you take it out on me?' Lily tossed back. 'How

is that fair? I've travelled for hours and hours, I'm tired
and hungry, and as soon as I set foot in the place I get
my head bitten off by a boorish man who has a massive
chip on his shoulder because he can't do some of the
things he used to do. At least you've got a roof over your
head and a family who love you, not to mention loads
and loads of money.' She put a hand over her heart the-
atrically. 'Oh, how my heart bleeds for you.'

His eyes were glacial as they hit hers. 'I want you out
of here by lunchtime tomorrow. Do you understand?'

Lily felt strangely exhilarated by their verbal spar-
ring. The atmosphere was electric, the tension palpable.
'Your loss, my gain. Well, I suppose it's your brother's
loss, really, but still. Easy come, easy go, as they say.'

He gave her a glowering look before he turned to
press an intercom button on his desk and spoke in French
to his housekeeper. A fine shiver lifted the hairs on the
back of Lily's neck as she listened to the deep timbre of
his voice in that most musical of languages. She wondered what his voice would sound like when he wasn't
angry. She wondered what his laugh sounded like. He
was such a compelling man to look at, so dark and intense, bristling with barely suppressed emotion.

'Dominique will show you to a guest suite,' he said.
'I will arrange to have you driven to the airport first
thing tomorrow.'

The housekeeper appeared at the door of the library
and escorted Lily to a guest suite on the third floor of the
château along a long wide corridor that was lined with
priceless works of art and marble statues that seemed
to follow her progress with their eyes.

'Monsieur Raoul's suite is that one there.' Dominique
pointed to a double-door suite as they walked past. 'He

is not a good sleeper so I did not like to put you too close to him.' She gave Lily a pained look. 'He wasn't like that before the accident. I blame that fiancée of his.'

Lily stopped in her tracks and frowned. 'I didn't realise he was engaged.'

Dominique gave her a cynical look. 'He's not. She broke it off while he was in hospital.'

'Oh, but that's awful!'

The housekeeper gave a Gallic sniff of disdain. 'I didn't like her from the moment I met her. But then, I haven't liked any of his mistresses. His brother's fiancée is another story. Poppy Silverton is the nicest young woman you'll ever meet. She's the best thing that ever happened to Monsieur Rafe. I just hope Monsieur Raoul meets someone like her.'

No wonder he was so bitter and angry, Lily thought. How heartless of his ex-fiancée to end their relationship in such a way. It was such a cruel thing to do. Surely she hadn't truly loved him? How could she? Loving someone meant being there for them in the good times and the bad. How could his fiancée live with the fact she'd abandoned him when he was at his lowest point? It explained so much about his attitude. It was no wonder he was so prickly and unfriendly. He was hurting in the worst possible way.

Lily followed the housekeeper into the suite that was decorated in a classical French style. The queen-sized bed was made up in snowy white linen with a fine gold trim that matched the gilt-edged paintwork of the suite. An antique dressing table with a tapestry-covered stool was positioned in front of an ornately framed mirror; there was a chest of drawers on cabriole legs and a discreetly hidden built-in wardrobe lined another wall. The heavily festooned windows overlooked the formal gardens of the estate where neatly clipped hedges, sun-drenched paved terraces and a large bubbling fountain were situated.

'I hope you'll be comfortable,' Dominique said. 'Dinner will be served at eight. I'm not sure if Monsieur Raoul will join you. He's not very sociable these days. He spends most of his time in his study or in his room.'

'How does Monsieur Raoul get up and down the stairs?' Lily asked. 'I didn't see a stair climber on the staircase.'

'There is a proper lift on the ground floor that goes to all four levels,' Dominique said. 'Monsieur Raoul had it installed a few months ago when his grandfather came for a visit after he had a stroke. Not that he got a word of thanks for his effort, mind you. Vittorio Caffarelli is not the nicest person to have around. He spoke to me as if I was the dust under his feet. I had to bite my tongue the whole time he was here.'

Lily was starting to suspect there was a lot more to the Caffarelli dynasty than she had first realised. She had read a bit online about the family—how they had made their wealth in property and a variety of timely and rather clever investments; how Raoul's parents had been killed in a speedboat accident on the French Riviera when he and his brothers were young. The three boys had been raised by their grandfather but had spent most of their school years at boarding school in England.

Raoul had been born to wealth but brought up with tragedy. And now he had yet another blow to deal with. Not that she had read anything of his injuries in the press, which made her wonder what sort of power the Caffarellis had at their fingertips. But how long would it be before some unscrupulous journalist came hunting for a story? It was certainly a juicy one: a rich man rejected by his fiancée after a freak accident that left him in a wheelchair.

In spite of her dislike of the man, Lily couldn't help feeling Raoul had been badly treated. Rejection was always hard, but to be cast aside because of injury went against everything she believed in.

What sort of money would be exchanged for a photograph of him now? Was that why he didn't want anyone he didn't know here at the château?

'It is a pity you aren't staying the month,' Dominique said. 'Even without the physical therapy you offer, I think the company would have been good for Monsieur Raoul. He spends too much time on his own.'

Lily found it ironic that she wanted to stay when only days ago she had been hunting for excuses *not* to come. 'I can't force him to let me stay. It's his call. If he wants to work with me, then I'll be happy to do it. But he seemed pretty adamant he wanted me out of here.'

'He might change his mind, *oui*?' Dominique said. 'You took him by surprise. Perhaps he will have a change of heart overnight.'

Lily walked over to the windows when the housekeeper had left and looked at the view over the estate. It was certainly a picturesque setting with its beautiful gardens and lush, seemingly unending fields beyond.

But the brooding man downstairs, who so resented her being here, reminded her that in any paradise there was always the potential for trouble and temptation.

CHAPTER TWO

RAOUL HAD PLANNED on eating alone in his room or not eating at all, but the thought of spending an hour or two with Lily Archer proved to be the greater temptation. He told himself it was because he wanted to keep an eye on her. Who knew what she might be up to when his back was turned? She might be pilfering the silver or stashing away some of his priceless objects while no one was looking—or, even worse, she might be an undercover journalist planted inside the château to get the prize shot of him.

He was still furiously angry with his brother for bringing her here. He'd planned to spend some time out of the public eye, working on his recovery as best he could. What could she offer that hadn't already been offered by his specialists and doctors? He wanted to be alone to get his head around the possibility that he might never fully recover. He didn't want people fussing around him. He needed time to process what had happened and how he was going to move forward.

Her understated beauty didn't fool him for a moment. That was probably all part of her artifice—to trick people into trusting her. Her nondescript clothing had hung off her slim figure as if she was trying to disguise it, and her brown hair had been tied back severely from her make-up-free face.

It was her eyes that had intrigued him, however. They were the most startling shade of blue, dark like slate, and veiled, as if she were hiding something. Eyes were supposed to be the windows to the soul, but he had a feeling Miss Lily Archer's soul was not for public display.

He heaved himself into his electronic chair even though it annoyed the hell out of him to have to use it. It made him feel even more disabled, hearing that whirring sound as he drove it. He couldn't wait to get this wretched plaster cast off his right arm. At least then he'd be able to keep his upper body in shape by wheeling himself around in the manual chair.

He caught a glimpse of himself in one of the large mirrors as he drove down the corridor towards the lift. It was like looking at someone else. It looked like someone had hijacked him and put him in someone else's body.

A dagger-like pain seized him in the chest. What if this was the best he would ever be? He couldn't bear the thought of spending the rest of his life stuck in this chair, having people look down at him—or, even worse, flicking their gaze away as if the sight of his broken body repulsed them.

He *wasn't* going to give in to this.

He *would* get well.

He would move heaven and earth to get back on his feet and he would do it like he did everything else: *on his own*.

Raoul was on his second glass of wine when Lily Archer came in. She was dressed in a long-sleeved beige dress that was a size too big and did nothing to flatter her colouring. Her face was free of make-up, although

she had put on a bit of lip gloss, and perhaps a bit of
mascara as her dark lashes seemed more noticeable than
they had earlier in the darker lighting of the library.
Her hair was tied back, but in the brighter light from
the chandelier overhead he could see it was healthy and
shiny with natural-looking highlights in between the
ash-brown strands.

'Would you like a drink?' He held up the bottle of
wine he was steadily working his way through.

She inhaled a sharp little breath and shook her head.
'I don't drink alcohol. I'll just have water... Thank you.'

'A teetotaller?' Raoul knew he sounded mocking but
he was beyond caring.

She pressed her rather generous lips together as she
took her seat to the left of his. Even the way she flicked
her napkin across her lap communicated her irritation
with him. Why hadn't he noticed how lush her mouth
was before? Was the lighting *that* bad in the library? Nor
had he noticed how regally high her cheekbones were
or the way her neck was swan-like and her pretty little
nose up-tilted. She had prominent brows and deep-set
eyes that gave her a mysterious, untouchable air. Her
skin was clear and unlined with no hint of tan, as if she
spent most of her time indoors, out of the sun.

She gave him a school-marmish look. 'I don't need
alcohol to have a good time.'

'So, how *do* you have a good time, Miss Archer?'

'I read. I go to movies. I spend time with my friends.'

'Do you have a boyfriend?'

Her face flinched. She covered it quickly, however,
adopting a composed façade that would have fooled most
people—but then, he liked to think he was not most

people. 'No.' Her one-word answer was definitive, like a punctuation mark. Book closed. End of subject.

Raoul picked up his wine glass and took a sip, holding it in his mouth for a moment before he swallowed. 'What's wrong with the men of England that a young woman like you is left on the shelf?'

She lowered her gaze and started fiddling with the stem of her empty wine glass. 'I'm not interested in a relationship just now.'

'Yes, well, I'm with you on that.' He lifted his glass to his mouth and emptied it.

She brought her gaze back to his. Her expression had lost some of its reserve and was now sympathetic. It struck him as being genuine; although he could have been mistaken, given he'd drunk almost half a bottle of wine. 'I'm sorry about your engagement,' she said. 'It must have been devastating to have it ended like that when you were feeling at your most vulnerable.'

Raoul wondered what online blog or forum she'd been lurking on, or whether Rafe or Dominique had told her the details of his failed relationship with Clarissa. He would be lying to say he wasn't upset at having been dumped. He had always been the one to begin and end his relationships. He liked to be the one in control of his life because—like his brothers—having control was an essential part of being a Caffarelli. You didn't let others rule or lord it over you. You took charge and you kept in charge.

No matter who or what stood in your way.

He picked up the wine bottle and recklessly refilled his glass. 'I wasn't in love with her.'

Her pale, smooth brow crinkled in a frown. 'Then why on earth did you ask her to marry you?'

He put down the bottle and looked at her shocked expression. Was she a romantic at heart behind that prim, nun-like façade? He gave a shrug and picked up his glass again. 'I wanted to settle down. I thought it was time.'

She looked at him as if he was speaking gibberish. 'But marriage is meant to be for life. You're meant to love the person and want to be with them to the exclusion of all others.'

Raoul gave another careless shrug. 'In the circles I move in, it's more important to marry the person who will best fit into your lifestyle.'

'So love doesn't come into it?'

'If you're lucky—like my brother Rafe, for instance. But it's not mandatory.'

'That's preposterous!' She sat back in her chair with an exhalation of disgust. 'How could you possibly think of marrying someone you didn't love?'

He met her gaze with his. 'How many people do you know who have married whilst madly in love and yet went on to divorce in bitter hatred a few years later? The way I see it, love doesn't always last. It's better to choose someone you have something in common with. Clarissa was beautiful to look at, she came from a similar background, she was relatively easy company to be in and she was good in bed. What more could I have wanted?'

She rolled her eyes and reached for her water glass. 'I can see now why she ended your engagement. Your attitude is appalling. Love is the only reason anyone should get married. If you love someone you will do anything to support them—to be with them through thick and thin. No woman—or man, for that matter—should marry for anything less.'

'So you're a romantic at heart, Miss Archer.' He

twirled the contents of his wine glass. 'You'd get on well with my brother's new fiancée, Poppy.'

'She sounds like a lovely person.'

'She is. Rafe's very lucky to have found her.'

The look she gave him was pointed. 'But from what you said just a moment ago you don't think their love will last.'

'I said love doesn't *always* last. I think in their case it will. For one thing, his wealth means nothing to her. She loves him for who he is, not for what he has. She is indeed a rare find. But, apart from her, I have yet to meet a woman who doesn't have dollar signs in her eyes.'

She visibly bristled. 'Not all women are gold diggers.'

Raoul nailed her with his gaze. 'Why did you ask for your payment up-front with a no-refund clause?'

She looked momentarily discomfited. 'I—I had an urgent financial matter to see to.'

'Are you a big spender, Miss Archer?' He gave her outfit a cursory glance. 'You don't appear to be, on current appearances.'

Her mouth tightened a fraction and her creamy cheeks developed two spreading circles of colour. 'I'm sorry if my lowly apparel offends your sensibilities, but I'm not a slave to fashion. I have other far more important priorities.'

'I thought all women liked to make the most of their assets.'

She gave him an icy look. 'Are you really so shallow that you judge a woman on what she is wearing rather than who she is on the inside?'

Raoul couldn't help wondering what she looked like underneath those dreadful clothes. He was used to women who shamelessly flaunted their bodies in front of him, wearing the minimum of clothes and the maximum of cosmetics to draw his attention. But Miss Lily Archer, with her dowdy outfits, scrubbed clean face and dark blue secretive eyes intrigued him in a way no woman had ever done before. She held herself in a tightly contained way, as if she was frightened of drawing unnecessary attention to herself.

Maybe you shouldn't have been so hasty to send her packing.

Raoul quickly nudged the thought aside. 'I try not to judge on appearances alone, but it's all part of the package, isn't it? How people present themselves—their body language, how they act, how they speak. As humans we have evolved to decode hundreds of those subtle signs in order to work out whether to trust someone or not.'

She began to chew at her lower lip with her small white teeth. It struck Raoul how incredibly young it made her look. It was hard to gauge her age but he assumed she was in her mid-twenties, although right now she looked about sixteen.

Dominique came in with their entrées at that point. 'Can I pour you some wine, Miss Archer?' she asked, glancing at Lily's empty glass.

'Miss Archer is a teetotaller,' Raoul said. 'I haven't been able to tempt her so far.'

Dominique's black button eyes gave a little twinkle as she placed the soup in front of him. 'Perhaps Mademoiselle Archer is immune to temptation, Monsieur Raoul.'

He moved his lips in a semblance of a smile. 'We'll see.'

The housekeeper left the room and Raoul studied Lily's almost fierce expression. A frown was pulling at her smooth forehead and her mouth was set in a tight line, as if she was trying to stop herself from saying something she might later regret. Her slim shoulders were tense and her right hand was gripping her water glass so firmly he could see the bulge of each of her knuckles straining against her pale skin.

'Relax, Miss Archer. I'm not about to debauch you with liquor and licentiousness. I couldn't do so even if I wanted to, in my present condition.'

She raised her gaze to his, her cheeks still bright with colour. 'Do you usually drink so much?'

He felt the back of his neck prickle with defensiveness. 'I enjoy wine with my meals. I do not consider myself a drunk.'

'Alcohol numbs the senses and affects coordination and judgement.' She sounded like she was reading from a drug-and-alcohol education pamphlet. 'You'd be best to avoid it, or at least limit it, while you're recuperating.'

Raoul put his glass down with a little thwack. 'I'm not "recuperating", Miss Archer. This is what I'm left with because some brainless idiot driving a jet ski didn't watch where he was going.'

'Have you spoken to someone about how you feel about the accident?'

His defensiveness turned into outright nastiness. 'I don't need to lie down on some outrageously expensive psychologist's sofa and tell them what I feel about being mowed down like a ninepin. I feel royally pissed off, or has that somehow escaped your attention?'

Her slim throat moved up and down in a tight little swallow but her eyes remained steady on his. 'It's understandable that you're angry, but you'd be better off channelling that anger into trying to regain your mobility.'

Raoul saw red. It was like a mist in front of his eyes.

He felt his rage pounding in his ears like thunder. What had the last few weeks been about other than trying to regain his mobility? What right did she have to suggest he was somehow blocking his recovery by holding on to his anger at being struck down the way he had been? Letting go of his anger wasn't suddenly going to springboard him out of this chair and back into his previous life.

The life he'd had before was over.

Finished.

Kaput.

'Do you have any idea of what it's like to be totally dependent on other people?' he asked.

'Of course I do. I work with disabled people all the time.'

He slammed his fist on the table so hard the glasses almost toppled over. 'Do *not* call me disabled.'

She flinched and paled. 'I—I'm sorry...'

Raoul felt like the biggest jerk in the world but he wasn't ready to admit it or to apologise for it. He was furious with Rafe for putting him in this invidious position. She was clearly only doing it for the money. It was ludicrous to think she would succeed where others had failed. She was a fraud, a charlatan who exploited the vulnerable and desperate, and he couldn't wait to expose her for what she was.

'Why did you take on this job?'

The tip of her tongue darted out to moisten her lips. 'Your brother requested me. He'd heard about my success with another client. My manager at the clinic encouraged me to take the post and the money was...um... very good.'

'I got the impression from my brother that he had to work rather hard to convince you to come here.'

Her gaze moved away from his as she picked up her spoon. 'I don't usually work with male clients.'

Raoul felt a pique of interest. 'Why is that?'

She scooped up a portion of the soup but didn't manage to bring any of it to her mouth. 'I find them...' She seemed to be searching for the right word. 'Difficult to work with.'

'Uncooperative, you mean?'

She moistened her mouth again. 'It's hard for anyone to suffer a major injury—male, female, child or adult. I find that generally women and girls are more willing to accept help and to work within their limitations.'

Raoul watched her for a moment or two, the way she toyed with her food and kept her eyes averted from his. Her cheeks still had two tiny spots of colour high on her cheekbones. Her teeth kept coming back to savage her bottom lip and there was a little pleat of a frown between those incredibly blue eyes. His gaze went to her hands—they were small and slim-fingered and her nails had been bitten down almost to the quick.

'You don't seem to be enjoying that soup. Would you like me to ask Dominique to get you something else?'

She met his gaze and gave him a tremulous smile but it was so fleeting it made him long to see it again and for longer. 'No, it's fine.... I'm just not very hungry. It's been a very long day.'

Raoul felt a faint twinge of remorse. He certainly hadn't laid on the Caffarelli charm he and his brothers were famous for. What if he allowed her to stay for a week to see if there was anything she could do for him? It wasn't as if he had anything better to do right now.

At least it would be a distraction from the humdrum pattern his once vibrantly active life had been whittled down to. What did he have to lose? If she was a fraud, he would expose her. If she had something to offer, it would be win-win.

'I have a hypothetical question for you. If I agreed to have you here for the next month, what would you do with me?'

A light pink blush stole over her cheeks. 'Your brother told me you have a gym here. I'd work on some structured exercises to start with. We'd start slowly and gradually build up. It would depend on what you could do. It's tricky, given you've got a broken arm, but I'm sure I could work around that.'

'What else?'

'I'd like to have a look at your diet.'

'I eat a balanced diet.'

She glanced at his almost empty wine glass, her mouth set in a reproving line. 'Yes, well, there's always room for improvement. Do you take any supplements?'

'Vitamins, you mean?'

'Yes. Things like fish oil, glucosamine, vitamin D— that sort of thing. Studies have shown they help in the repair of muscles and tissues and can even halt the progress of osteoarthritic change in your joints.'

He gave a bark of scorn. 'For God's sake, Miss Archer, I'm not arthritic. I'm only thirty-four years old.'

Her small chin came up. 'Preventative health measures are worth considering no matter what your age.'

Raoul pinned her with his gaze. 'How old are you?'

Her frown came back but even deeper this time and she seemed to hesitate over her reply. 'I'm...I'm... twenty-six.'

'You looked like you had to think about it for a moment.'

She gave a tight movement of her lips that didn't even come close to being a smile. 'I'm not keen on keeping a record on birthdays. What woman is?'

'You're very young to be worrying about that,' Raoul said. 'Once you're over thirty, or even forty, it might be more of an issue, but you're still a baby.'

She looked down at the soup in her bowl, that same little frown pulling at her forehead. 'My father died on my birthday when I was seven years old. It's not a day I'm used to celebrating.'

Raoul thought of the tragic death of his parents so close to his own birthday. Rafe had been ten; he had been eight, just about to turn nine, and Remy only seven. His parents' funeral had been on Raoul's birthday. It had been the worst birthday present anyone could imagine—to follow those flower-covered coffins into the cathedral, to feel that collective grief pressing down on him, to hear those mournful tunes as the choir sang.

To this day he hated having flowers in the house and he could not bear the sound of choral music.

'I'm sorry,' he said. 'What about your mother? Is she still alive?'

'Yes. She lives in Norfolk. I see her whenever I can.'

'You live in London, yes?'

She nodded. 'In a flat in Mayfair but, before you get all excited about the posh address, let me tell you it's got creaking pipes and neighbours who think nothing of having loud parties that go on until four or five in the morning.'

'Do you live alone?'

Her eyes flickered with something before she disguised it behind the screen of her lowered lashes. 'Yes.'

Dominique came in to clear their plates, ready for the next course. She looked at Lily's barely touched soup and frowned. 'You are not hungry, *mademoiselle*? Would you like something else? I should have asked. Was the soup not to your liking?'

'No, please, it was lovely,' Lily said. 'I'm a bit jet-lagged, that's all. I suspect it's affected my appetite.'

'I have some lovely *coq au vin* for the main course,' Dominique said. 'It is Monsieur Raoul's favourite. Perhaps that will whet your lagging appetite, *oui*?'

'I'm sure it will,' Lily said with a smile.

Raoul felt a spark of male interest when he saw Lily's smile. She had beautiful white teeth, straight and even, and her smile had reached her eyes, making them come alive in a way they had not done previously. He felt a stirring in his groin, the first he had felt since his accident. He tried to ignore it but when she brought her gaze back to his he felt like a bolt of lightning had zapped him. She was stunningly beautiful when she wasn't holding herself so rigidly. Her brief smile had totally transformed her rather serious demeanour. Why did she take such pains to hide her assets behind such drab clothing and that dour expression?

'I hope I haven't offended her,' Lily said once Dominique had left.

'She's not easily offended,' Raoul said with a hint of wryness. 'If she were, she would have resigned the day I returned here after my accident. I wasn't the best person to be around. I'm still not.'

'It takes a lot of adjusting to accept limitations that have been imposed on us,' she said. 'You want your old life back, the one where everything was under your control. But that's not always possible.'

Raoul picked up his wine glass again but he didn't take a sip. It was more to have something to do with his hands, which increasingly felt compelled to reach across the table and touch one of hers. He wondered if her skin felt as soft as it looked. Her mouth fascinated him. It had looked so soft and plump when she'd smiled, yet now she held it so tightly. She gave off an aura of containment, of rigid self-control.

He gave himself a stern mental shake.

He was reading her aura?

'That sounds like the voice of experience,' he said. 'Have you been injured in the past?'

Her expression closed like curtains coming down on a stage. 'I didn't come here to talk about me. I came here to help you.'

'Against my will.'

She gave him a challenging look that put a defiant spark in her gaze. 'I'm leaving first thing in the morning, as you requested.'

Raoul didn't want her to leave, or at least not yet. Besides, his brother had paid a king's ransom for her services. The no-refund clause she'd insisted on irritated him. She would be home free if he let her pack up and leave before she had even started.

No, he would make her stay and make her work damn hard for the money.

He gave her an equally challenging look. 'What if I told you I'd changed my mind?'

'Have you?'

'I'm prepared to give you a week's trial. After that, I'll reassess.'

Her expression was wary. 'Are you sure?'

'When do we start?'

She reached across the table and snatched his wine glass away. 'Right now.'

Raoul tightened his jaw. He knew he was using alcohol as a crutch. Normally he was appalled by such behaviour in others, but he didn't take kindly to being treated like a child who didn't know how to practise self-restraint. 'It helps me sleep.'

'Alcohol disrupts sleep patterns. Anyway, Dominique told me you were a bad sleeper.'

'I wasn't before.'

'Do you have nightmares?'

'No.' He could tell she didn't believe him, but there was no way he was going to tell her about the horrifying images that kept him awake at night. The pain he had felt on the impact would stay with him for life. The fear that he would drown before anyone got to him had stayed with him and made him break out in a cold sweat every time he thought of it. He couldn't bear the thought of being submerged in water now, yet he'd used to swim daily.

'I have a list of supplements I'd like you to take,' she said. 'And I want to introduce some aquatic exercises.'

Raoul held up his plastered right arm. '*Hello?* This isn't waterproof. Swimming is out of the question.'

'Not swimming, per se. Walking in water.'

He gave a disdainful laugh. 'I can't even walk on land, let alone in water. You've got the wrong guy. The one you're looking for died two thousand-odd years ago and had a swag of miracles under his belt.'

She gave him a withering look. 'You can wear a

plastic bag over the cast. It will help your core stability switch on again to be moving in the water.'

Raoul glared at her furiously. 'I want my *life* switched on again! I don't give a damn about anything else.'

She pressed her lips together as if she were dealing with a recalcitrant child and needed to summon up some extra patience. 'I realise this is difficult for you—'

'You're damn right it's difficult for me,' he threw back. 'I can't even get down to the stables to see my horses. I can't even dress or shave myself without help.'

'How long before the plaster comes off?'

'Two weeks.'

'You'll find it much easier once it's off. Once your arm is strong enough, you'll be able to do some assisted walking on parallel bars. That's what I did with my last client. Within twelve weeks she was able to walk without holding on at all.'

Raoul didn't want to wait for twelve weeks. He didn't want to wait for twelve days. He wanted to be back on his feet *now*. He didn't want to turn his house into a rehabilitation facility with bars and rails and ramps everywhere. He wanted to be able to live a normal life, the life he'd had before, the life where he was in the driving seat, not being driven or pushed around by others. The grief and despair of what he had lost gnawed at him like a vicious toothache. How would he ever be happy with these limitations that had been forced on him?

He could *not* be happy.

He would *never* be happy, not like this.

How could he be?

Dominique came in with their main course. 'Would you like me to cut the chicken into smaller pieces for you, Monsieur Raoul?' she asked as she set his plate in front of him.

'No, I would not,' Raoul said curtly. 'I'm not a bloody child.'

Lily gave him a reproachful look once Dominique had left the room. 'You're giving a very convincing impression of one, and a very spoilt one at that. She was only trying to help. There was no need to bark at her like that.'

'I don't like being fussed over.' Raoul glowered at her. 'I refuse to be treated like an invalid.'

'It's always much harder for people with control issues to accept their limitations.'

He let out a derisive grunt of laughter. 'You think I'm a control freak? How did you come to that conclusion? Was my aura giving me away?'

'You're a classic control freak. That's why you're so angry and bitter. You're not in control any more. Your body won't let you do the things you want it to do. It's galling for you to have to ask anyone for help, so you don't ask. I bet you'd rather go hungry than have that meat cut up for you.'

Raoul curled his lip. 'Quite the little psychologist, aren't you, Miss Archer?'

She pursed her mouth for a moment before she responded. 'You have a strong personality. You're used to being in charge of your life. It doesn't take a psychology degree to work that out.'

He gave her a mocking look. 'Well, how about I read *your* aura, since we're playing amateur psychologist?'

Her expression tightened. 'Go right ahead.'

'You don't like drawing attention to yourself. You hide behind shapeless clothes. You lack confidence. Shall I go on?'

'Is it a crime to be an introvert?'

'No,' Raoul said. 'But I'm intrigued as to why a young woman as beautiful as you works so hard to downplay it.'

She looked flustered by his compliment. 'I—I don't consider myself to be beautiful.'

'You don't like compliments, do you, Miss Archer?'

She brought her chin up. 'Not unless I believe them to be genuine.'

Raoul continued to hold her gaze, watching as she fought against the desire to break the connection. Her eyes were dark blue pools, layered with secrets. What was it about her that so captivated him? Was it that air of mystery? That element of unknowable, untouchable reserve? She was so different from the women in his social circles—not just in looks and manner of dress but in her guardedness. She reminded him of a shy fawn, always keeping a watch out for danger—tense, alert, focused. He would enjoy the challenge of peeling back the layers of that carefully constructed façade.

'What time would you like to start in the morning?' he asked.

'Is nine OK? It will be hard work, but hopefully you'll find it beneficial.'

'I certainly hope so. Otherwise my brother is going to be without a best man.'

She frowned at him. 'You mean you won't go to the wedding at all if you're not walking by then?'

'I'm not going to ruin all the photos by being stuck in a chair. If I can't walk, then I'm not going.'

'But you can't not go to your brother's wedding.' Her frown deepened. 'It's the most important day of his life. You should be there, chair or no chair.'

Raoul set his jaw. He was not going to make a spectacle of himself on his brother's wedding day. The wedding would be large and the press would be there in droves. He could just imagine the attention he would receive. He could already see the caption on the photograph: the poor crippled brother. His stomach churned at the thought of it. 'Your job, Miss Archer, is to get me out of this chair. You have one week to convince me you can do it.'

She moistened her lips with another little sweep of her tongue. 'I'm not sure if I can or not. It's hard to put a time frame on the healing process. It could take months or it might not happen at all…'

'That is *not* an option,' Raoul said. 'You've supposedly worked a miracle before. Let's see you if you can do it again.'

CHAPTER THREE

LILY DID HER best with the meal Dominique set before her but the intensely penetrating gaze of Raoul Caffarelli did no favours to her already meagre appetite. He made her feel threatened, but strangely it wasn't in a physical way. He had a way of looking at her as if he was quietly making a study of her, peeling back the layers she had taken such great pains to stitch into place. Those layers were the only things holding her together. She could not bear the thought of him unravelling her, uncovering her shame for the world to see.

She tugged her sleeves down over her scarred arms beneath the table. The multiple fine white lines were not as noticeable as they once had been but she still liked to keep them covered. She hated the looks she got, the questioning lift of eyebrows and the judgemental comments such as, 'how could you deliberately cut yourself?'.

But the external scars were nothing to what she kept hidden on the inside.

Lily hated thinking of herself as a victim. She liked to think of herself as a survivor, but there were days when the nightmare of her twenty-first birthday came back to her in sharp stabs of memory that pierced the carapace she had constructed around herself. Sometimes it felt as if her soul was still bleeding, drop by drop, until one day there would be nothing left…

She looked up from fiddling with her sleeves to find Raoul's hazel gaze on her. She had lost track of time; how long had he been looking at her like that? 'Sorry… Did you say something?'

'No.'

'Oh…I thought you did.'

'You looked like you were miles away,' he said.

She tried to keep her features blank. 'Did I?'

'Are you a dreamer, Miss Archer?'

Lily would have laughed if she could remember how to do it. She had long ago given up dreaming for things that could never be hers. She was more or less resigned to the bitter reality that she could not turn back the clock and make a better choice this time around. 'No.'

He continued to hold her gaze, watching…watching. She forced herself to keep still, to not fidget or shift in her seat. But the tension was making her neck and shoulders ache and she could feel a headache starting at the back of her eyes. If she wasn't careful it would turn into a migraine and she would be even more vulnerable than she was now.

Lily put her napkin on the table. 'Will you excuse me?' She pushed back her chair. 'I need to use the bathroom.'

He gave a formal nod without once disconnecting his gaze from hers. 'Be my guest.'

Lily let out her breath in a stuttered stream once she was inside the nearest bathroom. She caught a glimpse of her reflection in the mirror and flinched. There were still times when she didn't recognise herself. It seemed like another person lived inside her body now. Gone was the outgoing, cheerful, laugh-a-minute girl who loved to party with the best of them. In her place was a drab young woman who looked older than her years.

Lily knew it pained her mother to see her downplay her features, but it was the only way she could cope with the past. She didn't want to be reminded of who she had been back then.

That girl had got her into trouble.

This one would keep her out of it.

When Lily came back to the dining room, the house-keeper was clearing away the plates. 'Monsieur Raoul has retired for the night,' Dominique said, looking up from her task of placing their used glasses on a silver tray.

'Oh…' Lily wasn't sure why she felt a little tweak of disappointment. It wasn't as if she had been expecting him to entertain her. The fact that he'd joined her at table was surprising in itself, given how tetchy he'd been to find out his brother had brought her here. But to leave without even saying goodnight seemed a bit rude. Was it his way of showing her he was still in control of some aspects of his life? Was he reminding her of her place here? She was just an employee, one he hadn't even wanted to hire.

'Would you care for a coffee in the salon?' Dominique asked.

'Coffee will be lovely.' She stepped forward. 'Can I help you with that tray?'

Dominique smiled. 'You are here to work for Monsieur Raoul, not to help me. But thank you for offering. I will bring your coffee to you shortly.'

Lily gnawed at her lip as she made her way to the salon. Why had Raoul changed his mind about having her here? He had said he would give her a week's trial and then reassess.

But what exactly would he be assessing?

Raoul tried to concentrate on some bloodlines on the computer in his study. There was a thoroughbred sale in Ireland he went to every year, but how could he turn up to it like this? It was the most humiliating thing of all, to be so helpless that he couldn't operate his chair with both hands, but until this arm healed he was stuck with it. He had not realised how dominant his right arm was until he had lost the use of it.

As for his legs... He tried to wriggle his toes but it was as if the message from his brain was delayed. He gripped his thigh with his left hand, digging his fingers in to see if the sensation was any stronger than the day before, but it was still patchy and dull in some places.

He let out a frustrated breath and clicked off the website he'd been reading. He felt restless and on edge. He couldn't help thinking of his future yawning out before him like a wide, deep, echoing canyon. Long, lonely nights sitting in front of the computer, or drinking his way to the bottom of the bottle, waiting for someone to fetch and carry for him.

He knew he was better off than most. He knew it intellectually, but on an emotional level he couldn't accept it—wasn't ready to accept it. He wasn't even *close* to accepting it. He didn't want to spend his life looking up at people, watching them get on with their lives while his was stuck on pause. He was used to every head turning when he walked into a room. He and his brothers had been blessed with the good looks, height and build of their Caffarelli forefathers. He wasn't any more vain than Rafe or Remy were but he knew no one would look at him the same way while he was sitting in this damn chair.

He thought back to Clarissa's visit at the hospital. She had barely been able to meet his gaze, yet only days before she had been lying in his arms, her limbs entangled with his.

Now his limbs were as good as useless.

He punched his thigh, as if that would make the nerves inside wake up and take notice. He punched and punched until the heel of his hand was sore, but it made no difference. He raked his throbbing hand through the messy tangle of his hair, vaguely registering that he needed a haircut.

Emotions he had locked down centuries ago rumbled like the tremor of a mighty earthquake inside him. He hadn't cried since he was kid. Not in public; oh, no, not even in front of his brothers, especially Rafe, who had so stalwartly, so unflinchingly modelled courage, strength and stoicism from the moment they had found out they had been orphaned. He still remembered standing shoulder to shoulder with Rafe at their parents' funeral. He had been determined not to cry. And he hadn't. Remy had been sobbing out of bewilderment and Rafe had gathered him close. He had offered Raoul his other arm but he had shrugged it off.

Raoul had waited until he was alone to vent his feelings. He *always* went to ground when he had to deal with things. He didn't need people around, offering their useless platitudes and pitying looks.

But now he had Miss Lily Archer inside his bunker.

He pushed back from his desk and motored his chair to the door, but just as he was coming out of it he saw Lily coming up the corridor. She had her head down and her arms folded across her middle as if she was keeping herself tightly contained. She must have heard the faint whirr of his chair for she suddenly looked up and stopped in her tracks, her cheeks pooling with a faint blush of colour.

'I—I thought you'd gone to bed.'

'Not yet,' Raoul said. 'I refuse to lie down before eleven o'clock and even that's far too early for me.'

Her blush deepened a fraction but the tone of her voice was starchy and disapproving. 'I'm sure it is.'

'Are you a night owl, Miss Archer?'

'No.'

Her answer was so quick and so definitive. Every moment he spent with her piqued his interest a little bit more. What was going on behind the bottomless lake of those dark blue eyes? What was it with her stiff, school-marm formality? He couldn't help imagining her without that layer of dowdy, shapeless clothes. She was on the slim side, but even so he could see the jut of her small but shapely breasts beneath that sack of a dress.

What would she look like in a swimsuit?

What would she look like naked?

'Would you care to join me in a nightcap?' he asked.

She looked like he had just asked her to drink from a poisoned chalice. 'No.'

Raoul raised his brows. 'Surely one little tipple won't corrupt you?'

She compressed her lips until they were almost white. 'I told you before, Monsieur Caffarelli, I don't drink.'

'You can call me Raoul. You don't have to be so formal with me.' He gave her an indolent half smile. 'It's not as if it's me paying your wages.'

Her eyes moved away from his. 'I like to keep professional boundaries in place when I'm dealing with clients.'

'So you don't ever get on a first-name basis?'

She huddled into herself again. She reminded him of a porcupine folding in on itself to keep away predators. 'Sometimes, but not always.'

'So, how can I get you to relax the boundaries enough to call me by my first name?'

Her eyes were as chilly as a Scottish tarn as they met his. 'You can't.'

Raoul felt the thrum of his blood as she laid down the challenge. There was nothing a Caffarelli male loved more than a challenge—a seemingly impossible obstacle to overcome. They *thrived* on it. It was like air—as essential to them as oxygen. It was a part of their DNA.

He remembered the pep talk Rafe had given him and Remy when things had turned ugly after their grandfather had jeopardised the family fortune with an unwise deal with a business rival a few years ago.

Goal.

Focus.

Win.

It was the Caffarelli credo.

Raoul looked at her tightly composed features. She didn't like him and she didn't like being here. It was only about the money. This next week could be far more entertaining than he had first realised. He would rattle her cage some more and enjoy every single minute of doing it. 'Good night, Miss Archer.'

Her cheeks were still rosy but her eyes hardened as she raised her chin. 'Goodnight, Monsieur Caffarelli.'

He watched as she walked on past with brisk steps that ate up the corridor like a hungry chomping mouth. The door of her bedroom closed with a snap and the sound echoed for a moment in the ringing silence.

Raoul frowned as he wheeled back into his study. It was a new experience to have a bedroom door closed on him.

He decided he didn't like it.

Lily came down for an early breakfast the next morning to find Dominique talking to a man in his late twenties over coffee and hot, buttery croissants.

'Ah, Mademoiselle Archer, this is Monsieur Raoul's carer, Sebastien,' the housekeeper said. 'Or should I say, ex-carer?'

Sebastien rolled his eyes as he put his coffee cup down on the counter. 'I've been fired as of this morning. Monsieur Caffarelli has decided he no longer needs my help.'

'Oh…'

'I probably should warn you, he's in a spectacularly foul temper,' Sebastien said. 'I don't think he slept at all last night.'

'He's not very happy about me being here,' Lily said.

'Yes, so I gathered.' He gave her a sizing-up look to see if she was up to the task of dealing with such a difficult client as Raoul. 'His bark is worse than his bite, although I have to say his bark can be very savage at times.'

'I have no intention of allowing Monsieur Caffarelli to harangue or intimidate me,' Lily said.

'Good for you,' Sebastien said and, nodding briefly at the housekeeper in farewell, picked up his keys and left.

Dominique wiped away some crumbs from the counter top. 'Monsieur Raoul is not by nature a bad-tempered man.' She stopped wiping to look at Lily. 'You have no need to be afraid of him. He would never hurt anyone.'

'I'm not afraid of him,' Lily said. *Well, maybe a bit.*

The housekeeper's gaze held hers for a moment longer than necessary. 'He is in his study doing his emails. Will you take him his coffee for me? It will save my aching feet one more trip down that corridor.'

'Of course.'

The door of the study was closed and Lily stood outside it for a moment, listening to the sounds coming from inside. She heard the click of a mouse and then a vicious swear word in English. She waited another beat before raising her knuckles to knock on the door.

'Yes?' The word was sharply delivered, like a short but vicious bark.

Lily took a steadying breath. 'I have your coffee, Monsieur Caffarelli. Dominique asked me to bring it to you.'

'Then bring it in, for God's sake.'

She opened the door to find him sitting behind a desk that was almost as large as her bathroom back at home. He was dressed in gym gear, but it didn't take away from his air of authority and command. If anything he looked even more intimidating. His shoulders looked even broader in a close-fitting T-shirt. The stark whiteness of the T-shirt against the tan of his olive skin was another reminder of his love of the outdoors prior to the accident. She saw the carved contours of his pectoral muscles. His strong arms were liberally sprinkled with dark coarse hair that trailed right down over the backs of his hands and to his fingers.

Something shifted in her belly as she thought of those tanned hands touching her smoother, paler ones...

'Don't hover,' he snapped at her.

Lily set her mouth as she stiffly approached his desk. 'Your coffee.' She placed it before him. 'Sir.'

His eyes warred with hers for a tense moment. *'Sir?'*

She gave him an arch look. 'You don't like being called sir?'

'You're not one of the servants.'

'No,' Lily said. 'I'm a human being, just like you.'

'You're nothing like me, Miss Archer.' A flash of ir- ritation fired in his gaze. 'Apart from the obvious male and female thing, you're not currently confined to a wheelchair.'

'Perhaps not, but I am confined to this château to work with you for the next month,' she returned.

'A week, Miss Archer,' he said flatly.

'A week, then.'

A tight silence crackled the air.

Lily glanced at his untouched coffee. 'Is that all you're having for breakfast?'

He gave her a don't-mess-with-me-look. 'I'm not hun- gry.'

'Your body needs proper fuel. You can't ask your body to improve if you don't give it what it needs.'

His eyes glinted dangerously. 'What does *your* body need, Miss Archer?'

Lily felt the slow burn of his gaze as it lazily traversed the length of her body, a hot, melting sensation pooling deep in her core. His eyes lingered for a moment on her mouth, as if he was wondering how it would taste and feel beneath his own. She felt a strong urge to moisten her lips but somehow refrained from doing so. 'It's not my body that is the issue here. It is yours.'

'My body…' He gave a little grunt. 'I don't even recognise it when I see it in the mirror.'

'Muscle wastage is common after injury,' Lily said. 'We can work on that.'

His hazel eyes roved over her once more. 'Are you going to work with me in the gym wearing that dress?'

She felt her cheeks heat up again. 'No, I have a tracksuit upstairs.'

The sardonic gleam in his eyes was deeply unsettling. 'What do you wear in the pool?'

'Um…a bathing suit.'

Those wicked eyes glinted again. 'Maybe I'll change my mind about the water work. Who knows what delightful surprises will be in store for me?'

Lily pressed her lips together for a moment. 'I'm going to speak to Dominique about making you a protein shake. If you won't eat breakfast, then at least you can drink it.'

He held her gaze in that assessing way of his. 'Are you usually this bossy with your clients?'

'Only the childish ones.'

His brows lifted a fraction. 'You have a smart mouth, Miss Archer.'

Lily held her ground even though his green-flecked eyes were boring into hers. 'I speak as I find.'

'Tell me something…' He paused as his gaze continued to hold hers. 'Has that quick tongue of yours ever got you into trouble?'

She kept her spine straight and her shoulders neatly aligned. 'Not lately.'

A beat of silence passed.

'It won't work, you know.'

She looked at him blankly. 'Excuse me?'

His mouth curled up at one corner in a cynical manner. 'I can almost hear the cogs of that clever little brain of yours clicking over. You think if you're unpardonably rude to me it will make me send you packing before the week's trial is up. You want to take the money and run, don't you, Miss Archer?'

Lily wondered if he could read minds or if he was just much more cynical than she had realised. 'I don't believe in taking money I haven't earned. And, as for being unpardonably rude, I think you've already got the headmaster's prize for that.'

A satirical smile tilted his mouth. 'You're a spirited little thing under that demure façade, aren't you?'

She threw him a haughty look. 'I expect the only spirits you're used to seeing in the vacuous women you surround yourself with are the ones you pour into a glass.'

For a moment Lily thought she had gone too far. She saw his eyes harden and his jaw tighten. But then he suddenly threw back his head and laughed. It was a nice sound, rich, deep and melodic. It made the fine hairs on the back of her neck lift up and do a little jiggle. It made something that was tightly knotted in the pit of her stomach work its way loose.

Careful, the new girl reminded her. *Watch your step. Keep your guard up.*

Lily turned briskly for the door. 'I'll go and see about that protein shake.'

'Miss Archer?'

She turned and faced him. 'Yes?'

He held her gaze for what seemed to her an interminable pause. But, whatever he had planned to say, he left unsaid. His lingering smile gradually faded until it completely disappeared from his mouth and his frown returned. 'Close the door on the way out.'

CHAPTER FOUR

THE GYM WAS in a sunny room on the eastern side of the house. It was well-equipped, with every modern piece of equipment an exercise junkie could wish for. Lily trailed her hand over the state-of-the-art treadmill. She wondered if Raoul would ever use it again as it was intended to be used. He didn't look like the sort of person who would ever be satisfied to walk at a sedate pace. Those long, strong legs were made for hard physical exercise. She had caught a glimpse of his muscular thighs when she had run into him in the corridor last night. If he didn't—or couldn't—do specific exercises to maintain or increase strength, he would lose that impressive definition.

The change to his life was unimaginable. For a man who had chased adventure and women simultaneously, he was going to find any sort of restriction difficult to manage.

Lily thought yet again of his ex-fiancée. What type of woman was Clarissa that she could just walk away from him when he was struck down? It seemed so shallow and selfish. Raoul said he hadn't been in love with her, but Lily wondered if that was a way of dismissing or disguising the hurt he felt. How could he not feel some measure of hurt? It was like being kicked when you were already down.

She had seen many relationships flounder as a result of a person's injury. It wasn't just the injuries that changed people; it was the experience of confronting their own mortality. A period of reassessment nearly always occurred after a traumatic event. Relationships were either severed or secured, lifetime patterns were changed or adjusted, careers were either abandoned or taken in a new direction. It was a very unsettling time for the patient as well as their loved ones.

Was that why Raoul had locked himself away in his secluded château—so he could reflect on what had happened to him?

He was a complex man, deeply layered, with a keen intelligence to match those strong, observant eyes. It would test her sorely to spend the whole month with him. She couldn't help feeling he was toying with her, allowing her a week to prove herself, keeping her on tenterhooks, all the while luring her into his invisible web.

Lily turned when she heard the sound of his chair coming through the door. 'You have an impressive set of equipment,' she said without thinking.

His hazel eyes glinted. 'Yes, so I've been told many, many times.'

She felt her blush travel to the roots of her hair. 'Um… we should probably get started…' She hastily summoned her clinical professional self but she had never felt more flustered. Was he doing it on purpose, playing his double-entendre game so she would blush like a schoolgirl? All she seemed to do was blush around him. It was mortifying.

'Do you want me in or out of the chair?'

'Maybe we could have you sit on the weight bench,' Lily said. 'We can do some light weights and resistance work.' She swallowed tightly as he motored to the bench. 'Do you need help getting out of your—?'

'No.'

Relief flooded her momentarily. She'd been psyching herself up to touch him. She had lain awake the night before wondering what it would feel like to have those hard muscles under her hands.

She watched as he lifted himself out of the chair close to the weight bench. The muscles in his left arm contracted as he balanced himself. She could see the struggle playing out on his face. His mouth was set in a tight line, his forehead creased in fierce concentration as if he was willing every damaged nerve inside his body to respond. He finally sat down on the weight bench and visibly winced as he dragged his legs in front of his body.

'Are you in any pain?' Lily asked.

'I can handle it.'

'You don't have to be a martyr. Taking properly prescribed pain relief is not a crime.'

His hard gaze collided with hers. 'Can we quit it with the pharmacy lesson and get on with this?'

Lily let out a breath and held out a light dumbbell. 'Thirty reps, in three lots of ten.'

He gave the weight a scornful look as if it was nothing more than a dust bunny. 'Are you *serious*?'

'You can't go straight back to what you were lifting before. You could end up with even more damage to your spine. You have to start slowly and gradually build up.'

His jaw locked down stubbornly. 'This is ridiculous. I'm going to kill my brother for this.'

She put one hand on her hip, the other hand holding

the weight out to him. 'You can kill him later. Right now, you do as I say.'

He opened his hand resignedly and she dropped the weight into it. His fingers closed over it and with a little roll of his eyes he started on the repetitions. 'How am I doing?' His tone was unmistakably sarcastic. 'Can you see my biceps bulging?'

Lily was trying *not* to notice anything about his body, especially his biceps. She was having trouble accessing the professional therapist inside her head. In her place was a young woman who had not been this close to a physically gorgeous man for five years. It was hard to think of clinical specifics when a man as well-built as Raoul Caffarelli was sitting within arm's reach. She could even smell him—a hint of spice, grace note of lemon and lime, and a sexy understory of a man in his prime.

'Not so fast,' she said, hoping she didn't sound as breathless as she felt. 'You need to concentrate on the release as much if not more than the contraction.'

Those sinful eyes glinted as they tethered hers. 'I *always* concentrate on the release.'

Lily adopted a prim and haughty manner. 'Right; well, then, let's get working on your deep abdominal stabilisers. They switch off in the presence of back pain or injury. It takes a lot of work to switch them on again. You can feel them if you press a finger to your abdomen—like this.' She put two fingers to her own abdomen covered by her tracksuit. 'You pull them in like you were drawing your belly button back towards your spine.'

'I'm not sure I know how to do that.'

She let out an uneven breath. She didn't trust that

guileless look for a second. 'It's not exactly rocket science. You contract those muscles all the time.'

'Doing what?'

Lily couldn't hold his gaze. He knew exactly what activity activated those muscles. He had probably overused them in his marathon bedroom sessions over the years. 'Let's try some leg lifts. Have you any movement at all?'

'A bit.'

'Show me.'

He lifted his right leg an inch off the floor but it trembled as he did it. It was even worse on the left side. He could barely lift it at all. 'I guess I won't be running a marathon any time soon.'

Lily heard the faint hint of despair behind the quip. He was a man used to relying on his body strength. To have it taken away from him, or even reduced marginally, struck at the very heart of what he believed being a man entailed. 'Let's concentrate on getting you standing and then walking before we even think about running. Can you circle your ankles at all?'

He circled his right ankle easily enough but again his left was slow to respond. A look of frustration tightened his features. 'This is pointless. I can't do this. I don't *want* to do this.'

'You have to be patient,' Lily said. 'You can't expect instant results. This could take months or even years.'

His dark brows snapped together. 'Is that how you make your money? Stringing people along for years on end with a vague hope of a cure?'

'I try to be honest with all of my clients.'

'How about you start being honest with me?' He flashed his diamond-hard gaze at her. 'What are my chances? You can shoot from the hip. You don't need to sugar coat it. I can take it like a man.'

Lily ran her tongue over her sandstone-dry mouth. 'I think it's going to be a long and hard struggle to regain your full mobility.'

'Are you saying I'm *never* going to regain it?'

No one wanted to hear the bad news. That was part of the agony of rehabilitation. No one ever wanted to accept what fate and circumstances had dished out. Life was incredibly cruel at times. Bad things happened to good people. There was no way of getting around it.

'I think it's too early to say,' she said, taking the safe middle ground.

His eyes burned with acrid bitterness. 'You would say that, wouldn't you? It gives you a safety net in case things don't go according to plan. You get your money either way, don't you, Miss Archer? You've made sure of that.'

Lily bitterly resented his summation of her character. She was the very last person who would exploit another's vulnerability. She'd had her vulnerability exploited in the worst way imaginable. The memory of that night was like a cancer inside her head. She tried to radiate it with distractions, she tried to poison it with activity, but still it festered there, waiting for another chance to destroy her.

'I've had to put off several other clients in order to come here,' she said. 'Some financial compensation for that is not unreasonable.'

His green-brown eyes measured hers for a pulsing moment. 'Then we'd best get my brother's money's worth, hadn't we?'

Lily handed him a heavier weight, taking great care

not to encounter his fingers in the exchange. 'Yes. We'd better.'

He cooperated for a while but she could see his impatience simmering inside him. She knew it must be humiliating for someone so used to being in control to have so much of it taken away. But patience was exactly what he needed right now. There was no point going at things like a bull at a gate. Slowly but surely was the best way of managing any crisis.

She was living proof of that.

'I think that's enough for today,' she said, after he worked through a couple more exercises.

He frowned at her. 'Are you joking?'

'No.' Lily picked up the weight he'd left on the floor and took it over to the rack, trying not to notice the warmth of where his fingers had been. 'You've been sitting for more than ten minutes. Didn't your neurosurgeon advise you to limit sitting at this stage?'

'But I've done nothing.' His frown turned into a glare. '*You've* done nothing.'

'On the contrary, I've been observing you the whole time you were doing the reps. I was noting your posture and the activity of your muscles. You have a lot of tension in your neck and shoulders. Your left side is much worse than your right. It's probably a knock-on effect of the injury to your lower discs and, of course, your broken arm.'

'So what's the plan?'

Lily didn't care for the gleam that had so quickly switched places with his glare. 'Um…plan?'

'Are you going to massage me?'

A swooping sensation passed through her stomach.

Stop acting like an idiot. You've massaged hundreds of clients.

Yes, but none of them have been male!

The conversation went back and forth inside her head until she realised Raoul was looking at her quizzically. 'Is everything all right?' he asked.

'Of course...' She forced herself to meet his gaze. 'I'd need to hire a massage table. I didn't bring one with me. It might take a few days to get one. I should've thought, but it was all such a rush and I—'

'I have one.'

Lily gulped. 'You...you do?' *But of course he would.* A man who had everything money could buy would have a massage table. He probably had one for every day of the week. He probably had one in every room of his château. They were probably lined with gold or dripping with diamonds or something.

'It's in the room next to the sauna and Jacuzzi.'

'But of course,' she mumbled, not quite under her breath.

He hooked one brow upwards. 'You find my wealth something to mock, Miss Archer?'

Lily felt the scorch of his gaze as it held hers. 'No... I was just thinking out loud.'

'Then please refrain from doing so in my presence.'

Don't look away. Don't let him win this. He's trying to intimidate you. She held his steely gaze as each throbbing second passed. It was a battle of wills and she knew she was seriously, woefully outmatched but she didn't care. He was looking for a chance to wield some of the power he had lost. It was a game to him. *She* was a game, a toy to be played with until he got tired of pressing her buttons.

And he was pressing her buttons. Big time. Buttons that hadn't been pressed in a very long time—new buttons that had never been pressed before.

Like the one that was deep in her core. It felt like a shot of electricity went through it every time he looked at her with that dark, satirical gaze. Those glinting, *knowing* eyes were seeing much more than she wanted them to see.

She wasn't that wilful, reckless girl any more.

She was sensible and stable now.

She had her head screwed on tightly.

She had her emotions under control.

'What time would you like your massage?' *Had she really said that?* Lily heard the words but they seemed to have come from someone else's mouth. The new girl would never offer to massage a full-blooded man, certainly not one as dangerously attractive as Raoul Caffarelli. Her stomach nosedived as she waited for him to answer. The silence seemed to thrum with an extra layer of tension.

Sexual tension.

Lily smothered an involuntary gasp. Desire was something other girls felt. The new girl didn't have any place for such primal urges. She was literally dead from the waist down.

Or she had been until now…

'Shall we say eleven?' he said. 'I have some things to see to in my study first.'

'Fine. Perfect. I'll go and get set up. Don't rush if you get caught up with work or phone calls or texts or emails or anything. If you need to cancel, then we can always do it later.' *Much, much later. Or what about not at all?*

'I'll see you at eleven, Miss Archer.' A glitter of devilry entered his gaze. 'I'll look forward to a bit of hands-on therapy from you.'

Lily let out a flustered breath once he had left. Could this farce get any worse?

CHAPTER FIVE

LILY'S STOMACH WAS a frenzied hive of nerves by the time Raoul arrived at the door of the massage room. She could barely look him in the eye in case he saw how on edge she was. 'I'll leave you to get undress—I mean, ready.' She tucked a strand of her hair that had come loose back behind her ear and chanced a glance at him. 'Do you need help getting on the table?'

His expression was inscrutable. 'I'll call you if I need you.'

'Right.' She darted out of the room to leave him to it, her heart flapping like a sheet in a tornado inside her chest.

She came back in a few minutes later to find him lying face down on the massage table. She had left a towel for him to drape over his buttocks but due to his mobility issues he hadn't been able to position it correctly. It was a little skewed, giving her a good view of his tan line and the taut curve of his right buttock.

He is totally naked underneath that towel!

'Are you comfortable?' Her voice came out like a squeak as she carefully draped the towel back over him.

'Yes.'

Lily looked at the scar over his L5S1 and L4S2 discs.

It was still red and slightly puckered from where his neurosurgeon had operated to decompress the spinal cord but it would eventually fade to white.

She cast her eyes over the rest of him. He had an amazing physique—broad-shouldered, lean-hipped and well-muscled without being over the top. She could have stood there drinking in the sight of him for hours. It was so long since she had looked at a man—properly looked. He was like a sculptor's model, so beautifully put together it was almost painful to look at him knowing he was unable to walk or stand.

'I must be a whole lot worse than I thought,' he drawled. 'I can't feel a thing.'

Lily felt a reluctant smile pull at her mouth. 'I haven't touched you yet.'

'What's taking you so long?'

'Nothing. I'm just…um…getting to it.'

She drew in a little breath and pumped some oil from the dispenser into her palms to warm it. She put her hands on his feet to begin with—it was an anchoring touch she had used hundreds of times with clients. But never before had she felt such a high voltage surge of electricity from touching someone. It made her palms and fingers tingle as soon as she came into contact with his skin. She felt him flinch as if he had felt the same shock of contact. Then, taking another steadying breath, she moved her hands to his right leg, moving up his calf, working on loosening the tight, stringy muscles there. He flinched again and she heard him smother a curse. 'You can feel that?' she asked.

'Your thumbs feel like corkscrews.'

'Your muscles feel like concrete.'

He grunted. 'You should feel it from my side.'

Lily's mouth curved again. 'Stop whining and relax.'

She continued working on his legs, going up to his thigh and massaging with long, strong movements. She switched to his other leg and did the same. He was hard, hairy, warm and intensely male. His legs were powerfully made, strongly muscled and yet lean, without an ounce of fat on him anywhere.

She carefully lowered the towel from his buttocks so she could work on his attachment muscles. They were incredibly ropy and tight but after a while she felt them start to give a bit under her touch.

His body seemed to take a deep breath and then release it. She felt him relax into the table; his breathing gradually becoming slow and even.

Lily moved up his spine, careful to leave his damaged discs alone, working instead on the muscles and ligaments that supported them. He was tight in the neck and shoulders as she had observed earlier, but again after a while his muscles seemed to let go. His skin was smooth and warm, scented by the oil she was using and his own particular smell. It was a heady combination that stirred her sleeping senses.

She looked at the thick, black glossy hair on his head as she worked on his shoulders. Her fingers itched to feel it, to comb it, to tidy it. He had a tousled, couldn't-be-bothered-with-grooming look about him. She could see the traces of a style that was distinctly European—parted in the middle but long enough to sweep back over his forehead if the mood took him, the back long enough to curl beyond his collar.

Without even knowing she was doing it until she was actually doing it, Lily trailed her fingers lightly through the thickness of his hair. It felt springy, silky, soft and smelt like fresh apples.

'Do I have muscles there?' His deep voice was muffled from relaxation and from being pressed face down on the table.

Lily was glad he wasn't face up for he would have seen her fiery blush. 'No, but your scalp does.' She moved her fingers over the crown of his head, stroking and kneading to release the tension she could feel residing there. 'Do you get tension or cluster headaches?'

'Occasionally.'

'Migraine?'

'Once or twice.'

'What do you do to relax?' she asked.

'Is that a trick question?'

She felt that little smile tug at her mouth again. 'I'm serious. What do you do to unwind?'

There was a little silence.

'If you'd asked me that a month ago, I would have said sex.'

Lily removed her hands from his head and wiped them roughly on a towel. She didn't know what to say so said nothing. It seemed easier than making a fool of herself.

He turned his head so one eye could fix itself on her. 'Don't you find sex relaxing, Miss Archer?'

What could she say? That it was the most *unrelaxing* thing she could think of? He would no doubt laugh at her, make her feel silly, gauche and unsophisticated.

But then, if she told him the reason why she felt that way, she would have to confront her shame all over again. Stir up all those ghastly memories, set off a chain of nightmares that took months to go away.

Instead she snatched on the lifeline he'd inadvertently handed her. 'Does that mean you can no longer...?' She left the sentence hanging. It was devastating for anyone to lose sexual function but for a young man in his prime it was surely the most shattering blow of all.

'I have yet to find out.' He pulled himself up into a sitting position. 'The doctors seem to think things will be OK in that department.'

Lily was completely tongue-tied. She felt a fool just standing there staring at him. She could feel her face glowing with heat as the silence stretched and stretched.

'Don't look so shocked, Miss Archer,' he said dryly. 'I'm not asking you to rehabilitate me.'

'I wouldn't agree to it if you did,' she threw back quickly.

A glint of something indefinable entered his gaze as it tussled with hers. The massage room seemed suddenly smaller. The air thinner and tighter. Her breathing faster and more uneven. More audible.

She couldn't stop her gaze from drifting to his mouth. It was quite possibly the most sensual-looking mouth she had ever laid eyes on. She hadn't been kissed in years. She had almost forgotten what it felt like to have a man's mouth moving on hers.

Raoul Caffarelli's mouth looked like it knew how to kiss. A fuller lower lip hinted at the sensual power at his command; the slightly thinner top one spoke of a man who liked his own way and made no apologies for going out and getting it.

'Find what you're looking for?' His deep voice jolted her out of her stasis.

Her eyes met his briefly before falling away. 'I'll just leave you to—'

Before Lily could bolt he caught her loosely by the wrist. The Taser-like shock of his touch sent tingles down her spine. She looked at his darkly tanned fingers overlapping the slender bones of her wrist. If he so much as pushed up her sleeve an inch he would see the crisscross map of her shame.

She brought her gaze back to his, her mouth dry, her heart hammering like a piston in a faulty engine. Time seemed to stand still as she looked into that green-and-brown gaze. His lashes were thick and plentiful; his pupils were wide and inky black.

A girl could get lost in those eyes if she wasn't careful. 'You have a towel crease.' *Could you not have thought of something a little more sophisticated to say?*

His mouth slanted, making his eyes crinkle up at the corners in a staggeringly gorgeous way. 'Where?'

'On your forehead.'

His thumb moved slowly over the underside of her wrist as he kept her gaze tethered to his. It was the slightest, barely moving stroke, but it caused a tsunami of sensations to erupt like bubbling lava beneath her skin. She was acutely aware of how close she was to him. She was standing between his open thighs in an erotic enclosure that should have terrified her but somehow didn't.

His eyes went to her mouth. Stayed there. Burned there. Tingled there.

Tempted there.

He brought his gaze back to mesh with hers. 'Do you ever smile, Miss Archer?'

Lily moistened her parchment-dry lips. 'Sometimes.'

His thumb located her pulse and measured it. 'You're not very relaxed, are you?'

'I'm not the one who just had a massage.'

His smile tilted his mouth again. 'It was a good massage. Very professional.'

'Thank you.'

He slowly released her wrist. Lily could still feel where his fingers had been long after she had brought her arm back close to her side. It was like a hot brand that had somehow transferred its molten heat all the way to her core. She could feel it swirling there in a tide of longing. Needs she had ignored for years shifted, stirred, stretched. She felt the movement of it in her blood, the way her heart picked up its beat to keep pace with the heady rush of primal, earthy desire.

'Can you push my chair a little closer?'

Lily took a skittering breath. 'Of course.' She brought the chair to him. The towel draped over his lap did little to hide the unmistakable evidence of his erection. Her gaze seemed to be drawn to it like a magnet. She gulped. *Was it getting bigger?*

She finally managed to tear her eyes away. 'I'll just… go and let you get dressed.' She turned and bolted for the door, almost knocking herself out in her haste to open it.

Raoul watched her leave with a smile lingering on his mouth. She was an intriguing mix of sassy-smart mouth and shy schoolgirl. He couldn't make up his mind which persona he liked best.

You like her?

He looked down at the bulge of his erection. *Yeah, it seems I do.*

He pushed back from where his mind was heading, a frown rapidly replacing his smile. He didn't want an affair with anyone until he could be physically whole again. He could not bear the thought of a pity lay. He could just imagine the utter humiliation of it. Could there be a crueller punishment than to reduce a play-boy to that?

He was used to taking the lead in sex. He enjoyed sex. He had a strong drive but he knew how to contain it. He was a good lover. He wasn't selfish or self-serving; he wasn't averse to the odd quickie up against a wall or kitchen worktop, but only if the woman was with him all the way.

His gut twisted at the thought of never experiencing that primal power again. Even if he could perform he would be confined to doing it in bed. He wouldn't even be able to carry the woman to the bedroom. He would be old before his time.

He swore savagely as he reached for his clothes. If he still believed in God he would have cursed him, too. He had never been a violent person—not like his grand-father, who could fly off the handle at a moment's no-tice—but right now he wanted to punch his fist through the nearest wall in frustration. His mood soured like milk that had been left all day in the sun. It curdled his sense of humour; it made rancid every remotely posi-tive thought that entered his head.

You have to get through this.

How? He wanted to shout it until his voice cracked. *How am I supposed to get through this?*

Raoul eased himself off the table, but just as he was about to lower himself into his chair it moved out of reach. He made a grab for it but he only managed to push it further away. Anger and frustration surged like an erupting volcano inside him.

This is not my life.

I don't want to be like this.

He considered calling Lily to help him, but pride forestalled him. Surely he could get back in the damn chair without her help? It was only a step or two away. He held on to the table for balance, willing his right leg to move the short distance. He gritted his teeth and stretched out his hand. Almost there....

Raoul took a half-shuffle, half-hopping step with his right leg but his left leg wouldn't come to the party. It folded under him like a wet noodle and he landed in a crumpled heap on the floor, banging his forehead for good measure against the metal footplate of the wheelchair. The curse he let out cut through the air like a blade.

'Are you all right?' Lily called from the other side of the door.

He ground his teeth as he eased himself up on one elbow. 'I'm fine.'

The door opened and her eyes went wide as she came in. 'What happened?'

'What do you think happened?' He glared at her. 'I thought it'd be fun to look at the ceiling from this angle.'

She crouched down beside him, her slate-blue gaze concerned as she reached out to brush his hair back from his forehead. 'You've cut your forehead.' Her touch was as gentle as a feather and it made his skin lift up in goose bumps.

'Lucky me. A towel crease *and* a cut.'

She got up from the floor to fetch a tissue from a box next to the oil dispenser. She came back to him, kneeling beside him again, the tissue neatly folded into a square as she pressed it like a compress to his forehead just above his right eye.

His gaze meshed with hers.

A timeless moment passed.

Raoul could smell her fragrance—a light, flowery scent that was understated and yet utterly, powerfully feminine. Her eyes were like dark pools, fringed by sooty black lashes that curled up at the ends like a child's. Her skin was flawless, like smooth cream or priceless fine porcelain, her lips soft and a dark pinkish-red, just ripe for tasting.

He could feel her warm, vanilla-scented breath on his face. Her breathing had quickened, but then so too had his, along with his blood. It stuttered and then roared through his veins as his latent desire took a foothold and then pressed the pedal down—*hard*.

He slid his left hand beneath her silky ponytail. He heard the rapid little uptake of her breath and felt her hand still on his forehead, but she didn't pull away. Her lashes lowered over her eyes as she darted a quick glance at his mouth. He saw her moisten her lower lip, then the top one, with the tip of her tongue.

He applied the gentlest pressure to the nape of her neck to bring her closer to his slowly descending mouth.

He didn't kiss her straight away. He played with her lips with little pushes, little rubs and little teasing tastes, letting their breaths mingle and mate. She made a soft little sound, not a gasp, not a sigh, but something in between. Her lips were unbelievably soft and warm and tasted like the first harvest of sweet summer strawberries. He felt the shy hesitancy of her touch as one of her hands came to rest against his chest.

He covered her mouth with his, applying the slightest pressure, waiting for her to come back at him with the signal she wanted more.

She did.

He felt it in the way her lips softened against his, yielding to his subtle increase of pressure, opening like a flower to the first slow stroke of his tongue. He swallowed her little whimper and took the kiss deeper, tasting her moist sweetness, familiarising himself with the contours of her mouth, cajoling her tongue into seductive play with his.

She was tentative at first, holding back as if she was frightened of letting herself get out of control. But then the fingers of her hand resting on his chest suddenly curled into his T-shirt and her mouth became an urgent force against his.

He tasted hot female desire. It caused a firestorm in his blood, making him hard, thick and hungry for the slick, wet cocoon of her body.

He flicked his tongue against hers in an age-old rhythm that made her whimper in primal response. She moved against him, seeking more of him, her hands going to his hair, her fingers splaying across his scalp and then digging in as her mouth fed greedily off his.

He had never experienced a more explosive kiss.

It made every nerve in his spine—including the damaged ones—tingle in response. His groin was on fire. He felt like a teenager at his first sexual encounter. His control was shot.

He wanted her and he wanted her *now*.

And given the way her mouth was nipping and sucking at him, she wanted him, too.

But reality suddenly reared its head and its hand and slapped Raoul across the face. *What was he thinking? How could this go to the next step?* He couldn't even get up off the floor, let alone sweep her off her feet and into the nearest bedroom.

Besides, she was the hired help—the physical therapist who was supposed to get him back on his feet, not have him flat on his back while she rode him to Sunday and back.

His insides suddenly knotted.

Had Rafe set him up? Was Lily Archer and her holistic remedies his older brother's idea of getting him back into the saddle?

Raoul pulled back from her mouth with a muttered curse. 'OK, time to stop.'

She blinked at him for a moment. She looked vague, disoriented, shocked. 'Y-yes... Yes, of course.' She bit her lip and shifted her gaze, blinked another couple of times. Frowned. Frowned harder.

He watched as she scrambled ungainly to her feet, tucking a wayward strand of hair back behind her ear where the rest of her ponytail was confined. Her cheeks were pink, her mouth swollen, her gaze still averted. If he were to put money on it he would say she was currently feeling a little out of her depth, but he was not the gambler Remy was, and his money was staying right where he could keep an eye on it.

'Did my brother pay you to do that?' he asked.

Her bluer-than-blue eyes came back to his wide, startled. *'What?'*

He pinned her with a look. 'I know how his mind works. He's keen for me to get back to normal as soon as possible. Is that what he paid you to do? To test the equipment, so to speak?'

Her saw her slim throat move up and down over a swallow and her cheeks fired up another notch. 'I think you've got the wrong idea about me.'

'I don't need a bloody sex therapist,' he bit out as

he hauled himself up against the massage table. 'And I certainly don't need a pity screw to make me feel like a man again.'

There was a ringing silence.

'Excuse me...'

He turned his head to see her dashing out as if there was a fire in the room.

But then, in a way, there was.

His desire.

CHAPTER SIX

LILY WAS BEYOND mortified as she left the room, but angry, too. How dared he suggest she was here other than in her professional capacity? What sort of woman did he think she was? She knew the clinic had a bit of a reputation for being innovative in some of its methods but his assumption was nothing short of ridiculous! As if there was any amount of money that would induce her to sleep with anyone.

It wasn't going to happen.

Not for love nor money.

How could she be intimate with a man with those scars all over her arms and thighs? She could just imagine the look of horror, disgust and revulsion once her scarred flesh was uncovered.

The sad irony was that before her twenty-first birthday party she had been confident in her body, but that night had totally destroyed her self-esteem and taken away every scrap of her self-respect.

The cutting had been a way to release the emotional torment. It had been her way of controlling the shame that resided inside her body at having been taken advantage of by a man she had thought she could trust. Even though the rational part of her acknowledged she hadn't deserved to be treated like that, and the man in question had been very drunk, the emotional part flayed her with recrimination. She should have been more careful. She should have stayed with her friends. She shouldn't have drunk that fourth drink.

She should have told someone.

That was the one thing Lily had never been able to bring herself to do. How did you tell one of your closest friends that her older brother had lured you into another room and forced himself on you while everyone else had been partying next door?

So she had kept silent, and the pain and shame had burrowed deep inside her.

Which made what Raoul Caffarelli thought of her so totally laughable. Even in her partying days she had never been the type to sleep around. She'd only had two relationships—one when she'd been nineteen, which had lasted four months, and another when she'd been twenty that had lasted six. She hadn't felt emotionally ready for a full-on physical relationship.

Throughout her childhood she had watched her mother go from one ill-advised relationship to another, which had made Lily careful in her choice of partner. She often wondered if she had been a bit more streetwise if she might have been able to prevent what happened to her. Her judgement had been skewed by youthful complacency and familiarity.

But she was older and far wiser now.

And angry.

It was good to be angry because it stopped her thinking about that kiss.

How had it happened? One minute she'd been holding a tissue to Raoul's cut forehead, the next she'd been clutching at him as if his mouth was a lifeline. His lips had been like velvet on hers, warm and teasing, commanding and yet controlled. The seductive activity of his tongue had sent shivers rolling down her spine like runaway firecrackers.

You enjoyed it.

Yes, but that's beside the point. Kissing a client—especially one as dangerously, deliciously, lethally attractive as Raoul Caffarelli—was totally out of the question.

N.O.

No.

No!

Lily walked out into the gardens rather than hide away in her room. She needed fresh air and exercise to clear her head and to stop her body from its traitorous impulses. It had been years since she had thought about sex. She had become accustomed to pushing it from her mind because of the shame she always associated with it. But for some reason Raoul's kiss had not made her feel shame, but an intense desire to feel more of his touch.

He had been so gentle.

That had been so utterly disarming. If he had crushed her mouth to his and groped her with his hands she would have shoved back from him and given him a piece of her mind, if not a stinging slap across the face.

But she had been completely ambushed by his mesmerising lip play, the slow but sure stroke of his tongue, his measured pace, as if he'd known she would not like to be rushed or pressured.

It had made the hard, tight, locked away part of her soften and loosen. She had melted under the slow but sure seduction of his very experienced mouth.

She didn't like to think of *how* experienced he was. She knew enough about him to know he was a playboy, who before his engagement had moved from partner to partner with astonishing haste.

The sun was hot on Lily's head and shoulders as she traversed the expansive lawn that fringed the field where some magnificent-looking thoroughbreds were grazing. Their coats were like high-gloss satin, their powerful hindquarters shivering and their tails flicking every now and again as they shook off a fly.

It was a beautiful property with its rolling fields and lush pastures. But she wondered how Raoul was going to manage his arm of the family business while he was confined to a wheelchair. Breeding horses was a very hands-on affair. Attending sales and trials and track meetings would be next to impossible, or at least very difficult—maybe even dangerous. Horses were flighty creatures and thoroughbreds particularly so. It would be difficult for Raoul to have any sort of control over them when he was unable to stand.

One of the horses lifted its head from the grass and looked at Lily with big, soft, intelligent eyes. It blew some air out of its velvety nostrils and came over to the fence, idly swishing its tail as it went.

Lily held out a flat hand and the horse wobbled its soft mouth against her palm in search of a treat. 'I haven't got anything for you. I'll have to ask Dominique for an apple.' She stroked the mare's diamond shaped white blaze and then up behind her pointed ears. 'You're a beauty, aren't you? I wonder how many races you've won.'

'That's Monsieur Caffarelli's favourite brood mare,' a young boy of about fifteen or sixteen said as he came over from the nearby stables. 'Her stable name is Mardi.' He stroked the mare's gleaming shoulder. 'In her day she won all but two of her starts, didn't you, old girl?'

The mare gave the stableboy an affectionate nudge with her head before blowing out her nostrils again.

Lily smiled and gave the mare another stroke. 'She's gorgeous.'

'Do you ride?' the boy asked.

Lily dropped her hand from the horse's forehead, her smiling fading. 'Not in ages. I used to ride at a friend's country estate just about every weekend or during the holidays but we…we sort of lost touch over the years. I'm not sure I'd be very confident now.'

For months after her birthday party she had tried to keep her friendship with Georgina Yalesforth going but in the end the prospect of running into Georgie's older brother Heath had been too upsetting. One of the worst things about it was Heath had seemed to have no memory of what had occurred that night. When she'd next seen him, a few weeks after her birthday, he'd acted as he had always acted towards her—teasing and friendly in a big-brotherly way. All she could conclude was that he had been so heavily inebriated that night that—like so many other binge drinkers—he had no memory of what he'd done or who he'd done it to.

Lily had decided it was easier to sacrifice the friendship than destroy the Yalesforths' good name and reputation. After all, what hope did a working-class girl have over an upper-class moneyed family with a pedigree that went back two hundred years?

She would have been laughed out of court.

'You should get back in the saddle,' the stableboy

said. 'Mardi's quiet as a mouse. You'd be lucky to get a canter out of her.'

Lily gave him another brief smile. 'I'll think about it.'

'How long are you here?'

'A week.'

The boy glanced up at the château, his forehead heavily creased when his gaze came back to hers. 'Monsieur Caffarelli hasn't been down to the stables since he came home from the rehab centre. I don't think he's even come out of the château, not even out to the gardens. He used to spend all of his time out here with his horses. They are his passion. His life. But he refuses to come down because of the chair. He is very stubborn, no?'

'It's a very difficult adjustment for him,' Lily said.

'Is he going to walk again?'

'I don't know.'

'You must help him, *mademoiselle*,' he insisted. 'He is like a father to me, a mentor, *oui*? He got me off the streets of Paris and gave me this job. He's a good man— the very best of men. I trust him with my life. I would not have a life without him. You must *make* him get better. Monsieur Rafe thinks you can do it. So does Dominique.'

'Their confidence and yours is very flattering but I'm not sure what I can do in a week,' Lily said.

'Then you must change his mind so you can stay longer. I, Etienne, will talk to him, *oui*? I will tell him he is to keep you here for as long as it takes.'

Good luck with that, Lily thought as she walked back to the château gardens. Raoul Caffarelli might be a good man but he was one hell of an obstinate one.

An hour or so before dinner Lily went to speak to Dominique who was collecting herbs from the herb garden. 'Can I have a quick word, Dominique?' she asked.

'Oui, mademoiselle.' The housekeeper straightened from where she had been picking some tarragon.

'I was talking to Etienne down at the stables earlier,' Lily said. 'He said Monsieur Raoul has not been outside the château since he came home after the accident.'

Dominique gave a heartfelt sigh. 'It is sad but true. He won't go out until he can walk out. He is very stubborn when he puts his mind to things.'

'I have an idea,' Lily said. 'What if we set out dinner on the terrace overlooking the lake this evening? It's a lovely warm night, far too nice to be indoors. It will be a way of getting Monsieur Raoul out of the house without going too far. The fresh air will do him good and perhaps make him want to come out more.'

The housekeeper's black button eyes shone in mutual conspiracy. 'I have the perfect menu for alfresco dining. But how will you get him to come out?'

'I don't know...' Lily chewed at her lower lip for a moment. 'But I'll think of something.'

Raoul was in his study going through some accounts from one of his feed suppliers half an hour before dinner when he heard a soft knock on the door. 'Come.'

The door opened and Lily Archer stepped into the room. 'Is this a good time for a quick chat?'

He dropped the pen he was holding and leaned back in his chair to survey her features for a moment. She was wearing her usual don't-notice-me garb and her face was as clear and clean as a child's.

His gaze drifted to her rosebud mouth.

Big mistake.

His groin stirred and then throbbed with a dull ache of longing. Had he ever felt a more responsive mouth?

Had he ever tasted lips so full, sweet and tantalising? He could still feel the shy movement of her tongue against his. He could still feel the velvet softness of her lips as they'd played with his. What would it feel like to have those plump lips and that little cat's tongue sucking and stroking him on other parts of his body?

Don't even think about it.

He forced his gaze back to her blue one. 'It's as good a time as any, I suppose. What did you want to talk about?'

'I met one of your stableboys today. Etienne.'

'And?'

'He spoke very highly of you.'

Raoul lifted one shoulder up and down dismissively. 'I pay his wages.'

'He said you're like a father to him.'

'Probably because his own father beat the living daylights out of him since he was little more than a baby. Anyone who showed the least bit of kindness towards him would be a saint in his eyes. And there is one thing I am not, Miss Archer, and that is a saint. I would've thought what happened in the massage room earlier today would've firmly established that.'

Those two delightful spots of colour appeared in her cheeks. 'That was just as much my fault as yours.'

He gave her a levelling look. 'Because my brother paid you to service me?'

'No.' Her mouth flattened for a moment before she added, 'Because...I don't know. It just...happened.'

'It must *not* happen again,' Raoul said. 'Do I make myself clear?'

Her chin came up. 'Perfectly.'

A tense silence filled the corners of the room.

'Will that be all, Miss Archer? I have some important paperwork to see to before dinner.'

'That's what I wanted to talk to you about—dinner, I mean.' She twisted her hands together in front of her body, reminding him of a schoolgirl who had been summoned to the headmaster's office and wasn't yet sure of her fate.

'Then please get to the point.'

She gave him a brittle glare. 'You're not making this easy for me. Why do you have to be so...*beastly* all the time? I don't know why the papers say you're the most charming of the Caffarelli brothers. It just goes to show you can't believe a word you read in the press. As far as I'm concerned, you're about as charming as a venomous viper.'

Raoul drilled his gaze into hers. 'Have you finished?'

She ran the tip of her tongue over her lips in a sweeping motion that sent a rocket blast of lust straight to his groin. Her colour was still high, her eyes glittering brightly with antagonism. 'I suppose it's pointless now asking you to have dinner with me on the terrace.'

Raoul raised a brow. 'You're inviting me to dinner in my own house?'

'Not in your house. Outside on the terrace. Dominique's gone to a lot of trouble. It's a nice evening to dine outside.'

'Is this part of your therapy, to have me eaten alive by mosquitoes?'

She pressed her lips together for a moment. 'I just thought it'd be nice for you to have some fresh air. But I can see you're already made up your mind to stay inside and sulk and feel sorry for yourself. Fine. You do that. Have your own private pity party. I'll have dinner by myself.' She turned and stalked over to the door, her back stiff and straight as an ironing board.

'I'll strike a deal with you,' Raoul said.

She turned around and looked at him warily. 'What sort of deal?'

He ran his gaze over her primly pulled back hair. 'I'll have dinner with you out on the terrace if you wear your hair loose.'

Her eyes flickered with something he couldn't identify. 'I never wear my hair loose.'

He gave her a who-dares-wins look. 'Deal or no deal?'

CHAPTER SEVEN

RAOUL KEPT HIS part of the bargain. He used the manual chair even though it took him twice as long because he had made a promise to himself that he would not go outside until he could get there under his own power. Sure, it was bending the rules a little bit, but he'd made a deal with Lily and he wanted to see if she would take him up on it.

He transferred himself to the chair at the table Dominique had set up, complete with starched tablecloth, flowers and candles, and waited for Lily to join him.

He heard the sound of her light footsteps on the flagstones and turned his head to watch her approach. Her hair was longer than he'd thought; it swung in a glossy ash-brown curtain around her shoulders and halfway down her back. It had a bouncy wave to it that her tight ponytail had suppressed, and with her face bare and loose-fitting clothes it gave her an indie-girl look that was surprisingly eye-catching.

'You have very beautiful hair,' he said as she took the seat to his right.

'Thank you.'

Raoul couldn't take his eyes off her. She was so hauntingly beautiful, like a Tolstoy or Brontë heroine—

dark and yet pale, with that air of untouchable reserve. 'When was the last time you let your hair down?'

Something shifted in her eyes before they fell away from his. 'Not for a while.'

He felt an almost irresistible urge to reach out and thread his fingers in those silky thick tresses. He could smell the sweet summer jasmine scent of her shampoo. It teased his nostrils into a flare like one of his stud stallions taking in a new mare's scent. 'You should do it more often.'

'I've been thinking of getting it cut off.'

'Don't do that.'

She shrugged as if it didn't matter either way and picked up her water glass. He watched as she lifted it to her mouth and took a delicate sip. She was so self-contained it was fascinating to observe her. That little taste of her passion in the massage room had spoken to the primitive male in him. Her mouth had communicated what her speech and posture tried to keep hidden.

She wanted him.

He wondered how experienced she was. She certainly didn't look the worldly, confident type. At the age of twenty-six it would be unusual for her to be a virgin, but certainly not impossible. She'd said she wasn't interested in a relationship just now, which could mean she'd not long come out of one. Perhaps it had ended badly and she was waiting until she got over it.

Was that a broken heart she was hiding? She seemed a sensitive girl, in tune with other people's feelings. The way she had spoken to him about his break-up had suggested she had compassion and empathy for others.

The birds in the garden chirruped as they settled for

the evening. The warm air was fragrant with the clean smell of freshly mown grass. It seemed like for ever since he had been outside and yet it had only been weeks.

An ache tightened around his heart at the thought of spending the rest of his life indoors. How would he ever endure it? He didn't feel alive unless he was challenging himself physically. He loved the adrenalin rush of fighting his most primal fears in conquering a terrifying ski slope or climbing a vertiginous precipice. He had lived life on the edge because he felt grounded when he challenged himself physically.

How would he ever settle for anything else?

'Tell me about your life in London.'

'It's probably excruciatingly boring to someone like you,' she said.

'I don't live the hedonistic life the papers like to portray,' Raoul said. 'Compared to my younger brother, Remy, I'm really rather conservative. After all, I was about to settle down and get married.' He picked up his wine glass but didn't raise it to his mouth. 'You can't get more conservative than that.'

She looked up at him with those big dark blue eyes. 'Do you miss her?'

Right now Raoul had trouble even bringing Clarissa Moncrief's features to mind. He realised with a jolt that he didn't even know if her hair was naturally blond or coloured from a bottle. Had her eyes been grey or light blue? 'I miss being in a relationship. I can't remember being single for so long a period. But as to missing her... Not really.' *Not at all, if he were honest.*

Lily's brow was furrowed. 'Doesn't that strike you

as rather unusual, given you were considering marrying her?'

'I make a point of not needing people to that level. My theory of life is that people will always let you down if you give them enough room to do so. It doesn't matter how much they profess to love or care for you, there will always be a situation or circumstances where they will bail on you to serve their own interests.'

Or die on you and leave you lost and abandoned.

'But your brothers are always there for you, aren't they? Rafe seemed very concerned about you. He was so insistent I come here. I got the impression Remy was right behind him in that.'

'Rafe is distracted by his new life of love and his vision of happy-ever-after,' Raoul said. 'He wants me all sorted so he can get married and make babies with Poppy. But don't be fooled by Remy. He might show up occasionally and do and say all the right things but he only does it when it's convenient to him.'

'What part of your family's business does he work in?'

'Remy does investments and shares, as well as buying and selling businesses,' he said. 'He searches for ailing companies, injects funds and puts corporate strategies in place to lift the profile and profit margins, and then he resells them. He got into it in a big way after our grandfather lost one of our major companies a few years ago in a business merger that turned sour. Remy's made it his life's mission to turn things around and get justice, or his version of it, anyway.'

'Do you think he'll be able to do it?'

Raoul frowned as he reached for his water glass. 'I'm

not sure, to be perfectly honest. Rafe and I worry that it's going to blow up in his face. Henri Marchand—the man who duped my grandfather—is smart and incredibly devious when it suits him. His daughter Angelique is even smarter. There will be hell to pay and more if those two ever cross paths again. They hate each other's guts. I can't think of a person Remy would rather avoid than Angelique.'

'Why does he hate her so much?'

'I'm not sure…. Maybe he doesn't hate her as much as he thinks, but he won't admit it. If you think I'm stubborn, wait until you meet him.'

'Obstinacy seems to be a common trait in your family.'

'Yes, but in my experience it's the stubbornly determined people who get things done. Setting goals, working towards them, not stopping until you've ticked them off the list is the only way to get ahead. What's that old saying—if you aim for nothing you hit it every single time?'

'Yes, but not every goal can or should be achieved. It's good to set goals, but they should be realistic. Not everyone can be a Hollywood superstar or a billionaire entrepreneur no matter how much they hope or dream to be.'

He tilted his mouth at her sardonically. 'You're not much of a risk taker, are you, Miss Archer?'

'I suppose compared to someone like you I must seem very circumspect.'

'Do you ever push yourself out of your comfort zone?'

Her blue eyes moved away from his. 'Not if I can help it.'

He studied her for a beat or two. With her long hair

framing her heart-shaped face, she looked ethereally beautiful in the golden light of evening. He had never seen someone so completely unadorned look quite so achingly beautiful.

His eyes kept going to the soft, full bow of her mouth. He could still taste the warm wet sweetness of her in his mouth. He could still feel the shy play of her tongue against his.

Desire pulsed and then pounded in his groin.

She looked up and met his gaze as if he had summoned her with his errant thoughts. He saw the flare of female attraction; saw the way her cheeks were stained with a faint hint of pink and the way her soft mouth glistened after she ran her tongue over it to moisten it, as if she were remembering and revisiting the taste and feel of him against her mouth.

Lust burned hot and strong in his blood. He felt his body swell and thicken beneath the table. He felt the current of attraction tighten the air. He wanted her and yet he couldn't—*wouldn't*—have her. His grandfather's life-long penchant for sleeping with the hired help had made Raoul wary of indulging his senses to that degree. He liked his relationships conducted on equal terms. That was why Clarissa Moncrieff had been such perfect wife material. She came from the same wealthy background; there had been no fears of gold-digging motives because she had just as much wealth—if not more—as he did.

The realisation that he couldn't recall much about the last time—or any time—they had slept together troubled him. He knew he had made sure she'd been satisfied; he had some standards to uphold, after all. Mutual pleasure was the goal in all of his sexual conquests and he always stuck to it, even if some encounters were a little perfunctory in nature.

But the fact that he couldn't remember what Clarissa's kiss tasted like or whether she had ever looked at him with spine-tingling longing was a little disturbing if he were to be truly honest with himself. Being ruled by passion had destroyed many a man and he didn't want to add his name to the list.

Dominique came out with their entrées. She looked rather pleased with herself and exchanged a conspiratorial look with Lily before she set the plates down. 'Isn't it a lovely evening? Perfect for dining outdoors. So romantic.'

Raoul raised his brows at Lily once the housekeeper had left. 'Romantic?'

'The goal was to get you out of the château for an hour or two. There was nothing whatsoever romantic about it.'

'Why do I get the feeling my staff are conspiring against me?'

'They're not against you at all. They care about you, especially Etienne.'

Raoul looked out past the lake to the fields where his thoroughbreds were grazing. He could see his stableboy in the distance lugging a bale of hay to the feeder. That thin scrap of a kid who had come to him late at night on a Paris back street begging for food had turned into one of his biggest assets. Etienne had been brought up in filth and neglect; he had been distrustful of everyone and had hit out at every attempt to get close to him. It had taken Raoul months to get through the boy's thick, impenetrable armour. But now the boy ran the stables like a well-oiled machine. He had an affinity with the horses that was second to none. He preferred horses to people, and to some degree Raoul felt exactly the same.

Horses could be flighty or fearless, strong willed or biddable, yet once he had their trust they would do anything for him. It was so satisfying to see a willful, unruly yearling mature into a true champion. He had sold yearlings to racing syndicates from all over the world. He had bred winner after winner, champion after champion. He had been there from the moment his foals had taken their first spindly steps to watching them thunder past the finish line in some of the world's most prestigious races.

How could he possibly run his business from the sidelines?

But it wasn't just the stud business. He could not think of a worse form of torture than to watch a race while seated. No one sat down when a race was coming to the finish line. Everyone jumped to their feet—the trainers, the owners and the crowd. The cacophony of cheers and shouts as the horses came down to the line always gave him goose bumps.

How could he do it any other way?

Raoul met Lily's gaze. 'I suppose you cooked up this little scheme with Etienne—to lure me out here in the hope that it will make me yearn to get back down to the stables. But dinner on the terrace is not going to change my mind. I will not go down to the stables until I can get there on my own two feet.'

'I think you're being unnecessarily stubborn about this. Plenty of people run very successful businesses in spite of their physical limitations.'

'I don't think you understand what I'm saying, Miss

Archer. I don't want to run my business from a chair. I would rather sell it than do that.'

'But Etienne said the horses are your passion.'

'I have other passions.'

Her cheeks bloomed again with colour, but her voice was tart and full of spinsterish disapproval. 'I'm very sure you do.'

Raoul gave an indolent crook of his mouth. 'You don't approve of indulging one's passions?'

Her expression was tightly composed, almost too composed. 'Only if you don't hurt anyone else in doing so.'

'Have you been hurt in love, Miss Archer?'

'I've never been in love.'

'But you've been hurt.'

Her gaze skittered away from his as she reached for her water glass. 'Hasn't everyone at one time or another?'

Raoul watched as she took a token sip. So measured, so controlled, but behind that cool façade was a passionate, sensual young woman. He had felt that surge of passion against his mouth. He had felt the primal heat of erotic human contact, the mingling of her breath with his, the duelling of their tongues, the carnal desire he felt in her lightest touch.

He wanted to feel it again.

He dragged his gaze away from her mouth, his body still humming with the thought of bedding her. It was crazy even to allow the thought to enter his head. He was probably only tempted because it had been weeks since he'd had sex. Or maybe it was because she was such a fresh challenge to him. She had made it pretty clear she didn't like him or approve of his lifestyle. It could prove rather entertaining to change her mind.

Forget about it. You don't need any more complications in your life right now.

Raoul was getting dizzy from all the mental shakes he'd been giving himself. He wasn't in the mood for an affair even if his body thought it was a good idea. He liked to conduct his affairs with clear focus, with control and purpose. Diving into a fling just for the hell of it wasn't his way. Emotions were something he controlled, even though there was a part of him that kind of liked the thought of falling in love.

He and his brothers had spent their early years surrounded by their parents' love for them and for each other. It had set a standard, perhaps a rather unrealistic one, because not one of his relationships had even come close to what their parents had. Love and commitment had been central to their relationship. They still had their arguments, sometimes quite passionate ones, but they had never let the sun go down on their anger. Conflicts were resolved, slights forgiven, love restored.

Raoul had seen the change in Rafe, how falling in love with Poppy Silverton had given him an extra dimension to his life. Rafe had always been a goal-driven workaholic but now he was talking about taking extended leave for his honeymoon, and there were even baby plans afoot. Rafe had spoken of his and Poppy's desire for a family to love and nurture together.

Raoul knew his brother would be a fabulous father. He had been such a protective big brother, always putting Raoul's and Remy's interests ahead of his own. He had taken the brunt of their grandfather's anger countless times, even taking the blame for misdemeanours that Raoul or Remy had committed in order to shield them from Vittorio's harsh and unpredictable temper.

For the last twenty-five years Rafe had been the family anchor, but now it was time for him to launch into his new life. Finding Poppy—the love of his life—in a quiet little village in the English countryside had transformed his older brother into a man who embraced and expressed love with the same force of determination he previously used to avoid it.

You want that, too: love, commitment, children.

Did he?

He tried to picture it: a beautiful wife, two or three children, a dog or two…

A wheelchair.

His insides clenched and twisted at the thought of not being able to walk alongside his children from when they took their first steps or to walk with them into their first day of school. Not to be able to carry them in his arms, or to kick a football with them or teach them to swim, ski and water-ski as his father had done with him and his brothers.

If he had a daughter he would not be able to walk her down the aisle one day.

If he had a son he would not be able to stand shoulder to shoulder with him to teach him everything he knew about being a man.

It was impossible for him to imagine being a father without the full use of his legs.

He didn't want to be a father if he couldn't be a whole one.

How cruel was fate to snatch something away from

you just when you realised you wanted it? Raoul didn't want to spend the rest of his life pining for what he had lost. He didn't want to end up bitter and twisted like his grandfather. But how could he possibly settle for a life without the very things everyone else took for granted?

He would always be the one sitting to one side while everyone else was up and dancing through life. He would be the one everyone privately pitied or stayed well clear of in case the blow of fate was somehow catching.

'Are you in pain?' Lily's voice jolted him out of his reverie of misery.

'Why do you ask?'

'You were frowning so heavily I thought you must be uncomfortable. You've done a lot of sitting today.'

'I can hardly work at my computer if I can't sit or stand,' Raoul said with a fresh wave of frustration at his situation.

'Have you got a laptop? You could lie down and work on that. It would take the pressure off those discs.'

'I use my bed for sleeping or for sex, although lately I'm doing neither.' He scraped his hair back with his left hand. 'I can't remember the last time I slept more than an hour or two in one stretch.'

'Have you tried taking some sleeping medication for a couple of nights, just to break the cycle?'

Raoul gave her a quelling look. 'I'm not going to be turned into a pill popper, Miss Archer. Dependency is not my thing, in spite of what you might think about my current use of alcohol. I've only been drunk a couple of times in my life and both times I hated the loss of control.'

'I just thought it might help if—'

'You know what would help?' he clipped back. 'Being able to exercise properly. I like being physically active. I don't feel alive unless I get my blood pumping. I don't know any other way to live.'

She gave him one of her compassionate looks that made Raoul feel a brute for snapping at her. 'I'm sorry...'

He let out a muttered curse as he put his napkin on the table next to his plate. 'I'm the one who should be apologising.' Not that he was going to, of course. *He never apologised.* Besides, he hadn't asked for her to be here. It wasn't helping him one little bit having her to witness his pain and frustration. He wanted to be alone. He needed to be alone. 'I'm not the most convivial company right now.'

'I'm not here to be entertained.'

'No, you're here for the money, right?' Just like his grandfather's domestic minions, obsequiously pretending they cared about him just so they could collect their wage at the end of the day. He would be a fool to be taken in by her mask of empathy. She was just like everyone else, out for whatever she could get.

Her gaze lost its compassionate softness and her small, neat chin came up to a combative height. 'Unlike you, Monsieur Caffarelli, I don't have squillions in my bank account. So yes, I'm here for the money. I'm sorry if you find that hard to stomach but, quite frankly, if it weren't for the money your brother is paying me I wouldn't spend another minute of my time with you.' She put her napkin down like someone throwing down a gauntlet and pushed her chair back from the table to stand up.

'Sit down, Miss Archer,' he commanded.

Her slate-blue eyes flashed mutinously. 'Why, so you can continue to snip and snarl at me like a bad-tempered dog? No, thanks. I can think of much better ways to spend the evening.'

Raoul clenched his jaw so hard he felt his teeth grind together like granite against a grindstone. 'You will do as I say. Do you hear me? *Sit down.*'

She gave him glare for glare. 'I think I can see why your fiancée broke off your engagement. It had nothing to do with your accident or your injuries. It's your my-way-or-the-highway personality that's the problem.'

Had he ever met a more headstrong, opinionated woman? Raoul was used to people—and women, in particular—doing what he said even before he said it. Lily Archer was wilful and defiant and was a little too ready to express her opinions. Having her here reminded him too much of the power he had lost. She was rubbing his nose in it every chance she could. What had his brother been thinking, getting her to come here? The sooner she left—and to hell with the money—the better.

'Get out of my sight,' he ground out.

'See what I mean?' She gave him a pert look. 'You chop and change like the wind. You're moody and unpredictable. No woman in her right mind would put up with that, no matter how filthy rich you are.'

'I want you out of here by morning,' Raoul said through tight lips.

'Fine.' She gave him an airy thanks-for-that smile. 'I'll go up and pack right now.'

You just gave her what she wants. She wanted to get out of jail free and you just signed the release slip.

Dominique came out with the main course just as

Lily breezed past. The housekeeper turned and looked at Raoul with a crestfallen expression. 'What's going on? I thought you two were getting on like a house on fire.'

Raoul wheeled back from the table with an angry scowl. 'Don't ask or I'll fire you on the spot.'

CHAPTER EIGHT

IT WAS TOO hot to sleep. Or maybe it wasn't the summer temperature at all but rather Lily's overheated temper. She was packed and ready to leave, as Raoul Caffarelli had so rudely commanded, but a part of her was struggling with taking the easy way out.

To leave would be admitting defeat.

Raoul was certainly a challenge, with his forceful personality and stubborn ways, but underneath that brooding, angry and resentful exterior she sensed he was essentially a good man. Didn't his care and support of the former street kid Etienne prove it? He treated all of his staff cordially, if a little distantly. He had not said a bad word about his ex-fiancée, publically or privately, even though she had clearly hurt him by rejecting him the way she had. Didn't that suggest he was at heart a decent and honourable man?

He was angry and bitter and finding it hard to cope with what had happened to him. Lily understood that far more than he could ever realise. She had railed at the world, too. She had pushed everyone who cared about her away. She had felt so dreadfully alone but she had sabotaged every attempt to reach her emotionally.

Wasn't he doing the same?

What if she *could* help him? It seemed a shame to walk out and leave him to his own devices. Like a lot of men with an achievement-based personality, he had a tendency to overdo things, which could compromise his recovery. But he had more feeling in his legs than the Sheikh's daughter Halimah had at the start, and he was incredibly fit and strong.

But he had made up his mind, and she couldn't see him changing it any time soon. She had her money and that was all that mattered. It would be embarrassing going back to London so soon, but that was hardly her fault. Raoul Caffarelli would test an angel's patience, and she knew she was no angel, or at least not in his presence. He seemed to bring out the worst in her. She hadn't realised she had a sharp tongue until he had made her use it.

He was rude and arrogant and she was glad to be leaving.

Of course she was glad.

She hadn't wanted to come in the first place. Her life was in London. It might be a little predictable and boring at times, but at least she didn't have to deal with brooding, handsome men with foul tempers.

Lily threw off the bedcovers and padded over to the window to look at the moonlit gardens her bedroom overlooked. There was a swimming pool she hadn't noticed before in a sheltered section of the back garden. Its surface shimmered in the silver light of the moon, tempting her with its promise of cool refreshment from the night's sticky and cloying humidity.

It had been a long time since she had swum in public. The work she did with clients in the hydrotherapy pool at the clinic could hardly be called swimming. She spent most of the time standing waist-deep, guiding the client through a range of exercises. Her 'bathing costume' was a modest one-piece suit with a long-sleeved rash vest over the top, which she told her clients was to protect her skin from the chlorine.

The thought of a swim on a hot night in a secluded garden with only the light of the moon was a temptation she was powerless to resist. Given how reluctant Raoul was to come outdoors, it was reasonable to assume he wouldn't witness her midnight dip. It would be her way of putting her nose up at him one last time; her chance of having the last word. She would use his pool without his knowledge or permission and she would enjoy every minute of her little act of rebellion.

Lily picked up her one-piece and vest. Was it her imagination or did the fabric feel thicker and pricklier than normal? After a moment of deliberation she tossed it aside, picked up a matching set of bra and knickers and a lightweight cotton T-shirt to go over the top. If she was going to swim, then she was going to do it properly.

Once she was dressed in her makeshift costume she took a fluffy towel from her en suite bathroom and tiptoed downstairs, keeping an eye and ear out for anyone moving about, but the methodical ticking of the ancient grandfather clock on the second landing was the only sound in the silence.

The flagstones in the private section of the garden where the pool was situated were still warm from the summer sun beaming down on them all day, but the water of the pool was deliciously cool as she tested it with her fingertips.

Lily sat on the edge of the pool and dangled her legs

in the water. The splish-splash movement of the water against her legs seemed deafening in the silence.

She took a breath and slipped into the cool, silky embrace of the water. It lifted the hairs from her scalp, playing with them in a watery dance that made her aware of every inch of her flesh. She duck dived to the bottom of the pool and swam like a mermaid with dolphin-like undulations of her body, feeling free in a way she hadn't felt in years.

She came back up to the surface and swam lap after lap, the rhythmic movement of her limbs lulling her into a state of calm that was both meditative and incredibly soothing.

She had no idea how far or for how long she had been swimming. She had made a vain attempt to count her laps in the beginning, but her mind had drifted into blissful numbness after the first ten or so. She was totally in the moment, feeling the water move over her skin, feeling the contraction and pull of her muscles as she carved through the resistance of the cool, refreshing fluid that surrounded her. She was weightless, yet strong. Her body felt invigorated, tired yet satisfied, her blood singing around her veins in delight at being active after spending so much time indoors.

Lily finally surfaced at one end and threw back the long wet curtain of her hair. But when she opened her eyes she found Raoul sitting in his chair watching her from the side of the pool with an inscrutable expression on his face. Her heart gave a little stutter in her chest but it had nothing to do with the physical exertion she had just performed. 'How long have you been there?' she asked.

'Long enough.'

She focused her gaze on the tiles near her hands rather than meet his gaze. 'I suppose you're thinking what a totally rubbish swimmer I am.'

'On the contrary, you look quite at home in the water. But that T-shirt must be annoying. It's creating quite a drag when you swim.'

Lily met his gaze with a little hitch of her chin. 'I don't like swimming in public.'

He arched a dark brow in a wry manner. 'It's hardly *public* out here.'

'*You're* here.'

His gaze slowly but surely moved over her like a minesweeper, detonating all of her senses in the process. 'Wasn't that your goal, to get me outside of the château?'

She wrapped her arms around her body, hoping the light wasn't good enough for him to see her in too much detail. 'I want to get out. I'm getting cold.'

'So?'

'So you need to leave.'

His dark eyes did another lazy sweep of her upper body, lingering for a moment on the upthrust of her breasts where her crossed-over arms had showcased them as good as any push-up bra. Her flesh tingled where his gaze had rested. It felt like a fire had been lit beneath her skin.

'Last time I looked, this was my château and my pool. If anyone is trespassing it is you.'

Lily set her mouth. 'I'm not getting out until you leave.'

He gave her a devil-may-care smile, his hazel eyes glinting. 'I'm not leaving until you get out.'

The water hadn't seemed cold until he had laid down that challenge. Goose bumps peppered all over her body as she tried to stare him down. Her T-shirt clung to her like a wet sheet and she knew that right at this moment it was probably showing far more than she was trying to hide.

Was the moonlight muted enough that he wouldn't see the roadmap of her pain on her arms? What did it matter if he *did* see it? It wasn't as if she were trying to impress him. She was leaving at first light. She had packed all her things and was ready to go. Dominique had slipped the flight details he had booked under her door only a couple of hours ago.

'Could you pass me my towel?' It was a form of compromise but there was no way Lily was going to let him win this battle.

'Swim a lap without the T-shirt.'

'Pardon?'

His eyes trapped hers. 'Take it off.'

She felt a traitorous frisson pass over her flesh at his authoritative tone. 'I'll take it off if you join me in the water.' As soon as she issued the challenge, she regretted it. *What was she thinking?* He loved a challenge. Didn't she know that by now?

'Nice one.' He gave her a gleaming half smile. 'Clever. Tactical.'

'So...' She swallowed. 'You'll do it?' *Don't do it! Don't do it!*

He moved his chair closer to the side of the pool. His eyes stayed on hers as he unbuttoned his shirt. Her breath stalled as each inch of his chest was revealed. He shrugged himself out of his shirt and tossed it to one side.

Lily gulped as he started on the waistband of his trousers. Was he really going to join her in the water? *Yikes!*

'Um…maybe this is not such a great idea. What about your plaster cast? It'll get soak—'

'I'll get another one put on if it gets wet. Anyway, it's almost time it came off. What's a couple of weeks?'

'You can't just ignore your doctor's orders to do what you like.'

'Water therapy was part of your plan for me, wasn't it?'

'Yes, but you told me you didn't want me to stay,' Lily quickly reminded him. 'I'm officially off duty. You terminated my contract. I don't have to do anything with you if I don't want to— What are you *doing*?'

'I'm getting undressed.'

Lily clamped her hands over her eyes. 'You can't do that!'

'I always swim naked when I'm at home. It's totally private here.'

'But I can see you!'

'So?'

She stole a little peek from between her fingers. 'I don't want to see you.'

'Then don't look.'

How could she *not* look? He looked like he had just stepped down off a plinth in the Louvre, so beautifully carved and sculptured. Everything about him spoke of a man in the prime of his life, strong, virile and staggeringly potent if the proud heft of him beneath the black underwear he was wearing was any indication.

Was he going to take them off?

She opened her fingers a tiny bit wider. The muscles of his left arm bunched as they took his weight as he eased out of the chair but he left his underwear on. She wondered if peeling them off would be too difficult in the chair. Maybe once he was in the water...

Eek! He was in the water!

Lily snatched in a breath as the water his body displaced when he entered the pool moved across her breast like a liquid caress. Her nipples reacted as if he had touched them, tight and aching, so sensitive she could feel them pushing against the lace of her sodden bra.

Her belly quivered as she roved her gaze over his chest. He had the broad and well-defined shoulders and biceps of a regular swimmer. His chest was generously covered with coarse masculine hair that spread from a wide T across his pectoral muscles, narrowing down over the washboard of his flat abdomen to disappear—rather tantalisingly, she thought—beneath his hip-hugging briefs.

OK, my girl, remember that pair of lungs inside your chest? They're for breathing.

Lily drew in a breath but it fluttered against her windpipe like the wings of a moth trapped inside a straw. Her heart was doing a crazy little pitter-pat pitter-pat behind her ribcage and the desire she thought had been dead and buried long ago reared its head and screamed, *I'm alive!*

He was holding on to the side of the pool with his left arm while he kept his other raised just above the water. He moved along the wall until he was in the deeper end so the water could support him, but even so his head and shoulders easily cleared the surface. For the first time Lily got a sense of how tall he was. She wouldn't come up to his chin in her bare feet.

'How does it feel?' she asked.

'Wet.'

Lily couldn't read his expression, as he was in the

shadow cast by the nearby shrubbery, but she got the sense he was not totally at ease being back in the water. She wondered if it was bringing back horrible memories of his accident. A water-based accident always held the terrifying prospect of drowning. How soon had help come to him? How long had he floundered with his arm broken and his spine damaged?

But a challenge was a challenge and he was clearly taking her up on it.

She moved closer to him, her legs treading water to keep her afloat as she got within touching distance. 'Do you need a hand?'

'Right now a pair of legs would be quite handy. The ones I've got don't seem to be working all that well.'

'Can you move them at all? Sometimes the water helps you become more aware of your body.'

'I'm aware of it, all right.'

This time Lily could see his expression and her belly gave another little swoop and dive at the glitter of male desire shining there. She was aware of his body, too.

Very aware.

One of her legs brushed against one of his underneath the water. It sent a shockwave of fizzing sensations all the way to her core.

His gaze went to her mouth, lingering there for a heart-stopping moment before ensnaring hers once more. 'So, you've got me outside and now you've got me in the water. What's the next step in your plan?'

She gave him an arch look. 'I get you to apologise.'

'For what?'

'For telling me to get out of your sight.'

His eyes measured hers for a pulsing moment. She could see the battle playing out on his features: the tiny twitch of a muscle near the corner of his mouth; the tensing of his jaw; the set of his lips into a tight line; the fissure of a frown between his black eyebrows.

'I never wanted you here in the first place.'

'There are much better ways of telling a person their services are no longer required than dismissing them from the table like a misbehaving child,' she tossed back.

'You overstepped the mark.'

'Because I dared to criticise your personality?'

'No.' His eyes were as hard as diamonds. 'Because you wouldn't do as I said.'

'I'm sure you're used to people bowing and scraping to you because you've got truckloads of money, but in my opinion respect has to be earned, not bought. And, just for the record, I don't take orders and I won't be bullied into obedience.'

'We seem to be at somewhat of an impasse, Miss Archer, for I won't apologise and you won't take an order.'

Lily didn't back down even though his look was long and steely and the set to his mouth determined. 'It won't matter come tomorrow. I'll be leaving, as per your instructions. And, let me tell you, I'm *very* glad to be going. Glad, glad, glad. Ecstatic, actually.'

'Of course you are.' His top lip curled in that mocking way he had perfected. 'You've been looking for an escape route from the first moment you arrived. I'm playing right into your hands by telling you to leave.'

Then why did it feel so wrong to be going? 'You're not my preferred type of client.'

'Because I'm male?'

'Because you're arrogant and insufferably rude.'

The warm night air sizzled with electricity as his green-and-brown gaze held hers in silent combat. But it seemed much more than a simple battle of wills. Lily was intensely aware that the same water that surrounded and touched her body was surrounding and touching his. It added a level of intimacy that was disturbing and yet exciting at the same time.

'Why are you wearing a T-shirt?'

The question coming out of the silence threw her for a moment. 'I—I have very sensitive skin.'

'The moon doesn't have UV rays.'

She gave him a withering look as she folded her arms across her chest. 'Ha ha.'

His eyes grazed the shape of her breasts and then narrowed as they came to rest on her forearms. His gaze came back to hers, dark and concerned. 'What happened to your arms?'

Lily dropped her arms back down below the water. 'Nothing.'

'Doesn't look like nothing to me. It looks like you got up close and personal with a razor blade. Did you need stitches?'

'No.'

'Hospitalisation?'

Lily compressed her lips. She didn't want to talk about that time in her life. She didn't want to have to explain why she had felt so compelled to do what she had done. She just wanted to put it all behind her and move on.

She *had* moved on.

'Did you cut anywhere else?' His voice was gentle now rather than judgemental, which totally surprised her. Disarmed her.

She let out a breath of resignation. She was leaving

in the morning; he could think what he liked of her.
'My thighs.'

He winced as if he had personally felt each and every
slice of the blades that had marked her flesh. 'What happened to you?'

'I bled. A lot.'

'Not when you cut.' He frowned at her attempt at
black humour. 'What happened to make you want to
do that?'

Lily put on her tough-as-nails face. 'I was a bit messed
up a few years ago. I took it out on myself. Not a great
way of handling things, but still.'

'Drugs?'

'No.'

'Relationship problems?'

She gave a little cough of humourless laughter. 'You
could say that.'

'Do you want to talk about it?'

'No.'

'Do you still cut?'

Lily flashed him an irritated look. 'No, of course not.'

He held her gaze for longer than she felt comfortable
with. He seemed to be seeing right through her façade.

It terrified her.

'I'd like to get out of the pool.' She gave him a haughty
look. 'Do I have to ask permission or are you going to
stand there and watch me freeze to death?'

'I'm not standing,' he pointed out wryly. 'I'm leaning. And you're not freezing, you're scared.'

She raised her chin. 'Not of you.'

His gaze held hers in that quietly assessing way that
unsettled her so much. 'I'm very glad to hear it. How
could we ever work together if you're frightened of me?'

Lily blinked at him. 'You want to work with me?'

'Yes.'

'But… But I thought…?'

'I'd like you to stay for the month. I'll pay you double the amount my brother offered.'

She looked at him in bafflement. Why had he changed his mind? Hadn't her scars put him off? Most people shunned her when they saw her body. He was doing the opposite.

Why?

Who cares? Think of the money. Two years' wages for a month's work!

'But I don't understand…'

'I quite like the idea of getting to know you, Lily Archer. I suspect no one else has achieved that before.'

She gave him a guarded look. 'I suppose you see me as yet another challenge to overcome?'

'No.' His eyes glanced briefly at her mouth before coming back to mesh with hers. 'I see you as a temptation I should resist.'

Her brows lifted. 'Should?'

'Can't,' he said, and before she could move even an inch out of his way he covered her mouth with his.

CHAPTER NINE

THE FEEL OF his mouth on hers made every nerve in Lily's body stand up and quiver in delight. He tasted of mint and male heat, an intoxicating blend that made her senses spin out of control. His tongue found hers and called it into an erotic dance that made her insides do a series of frantic somersaults. It was a much harder kiss than his previous one, more focused, even more ruthlessly determined.

Even more irresistible.

His body was flush against hers, his erection pressing against her stomach. It burned like a brand against her, the primitive need it signalled calling out to her own. She felt the tingling of her desire deep in her pelvis, the throb-ache pulse that pounded in time with her blood.

Had she ever experienced sexual attraction like this before? If so, she couldn't remember it, and nor could her body. It was as if she were experiencing desire for the very first time. Never before had her body felt so in tune with a man's touch. She had never felt a need so strong she couldn't find an excuse to delay its satiation. She softened against him like molten wax against a source of heat, her legs entwining with his.

Male against female, light against dark. It was a po-

tent mix of hormones and needs that swirled and sim-
mered in the water that enveloped them.

She wanted more.

She wanted to feel his hands and mouth on her
breasts. She was so out of practice she didn't know how
to communicate her need. She made a little mewling
sound against his lips, pressing closer; conscious he was
only supporting himself with his one good arm.

He kissed her again, slowly first, and then deeply
and passionately. She tasted the need that was thunder-
ing through his body. It called to everything that was
female in her. She kissed him back with such fervour it
made her heart race to think he wanted her even half as
much as she wanted him.

Somehow they got to the steps so he could sit and
she could stand between his open thighs. He cupped
her breast with a gentle hand, his thumb rolling over the
pebbled nipple as his mouth savoured hers in little nips,
sucks and licks that thrilled her senses. Whatever fear
or trepidation she had felt had completely dissipated.
All she could feel was the desire for completion. It was
a bone-deep ache that made her blood hum inside the
circuitry of her veins.

He lifted his mouth just a fraction off hers, his voice
low, deep and sexy. 'I want to make love to you.'

Lily suddenly realised the implications of what she
was doing. Where was her professionalism? Where was
her self-control? What was she thinking, kissing Raoul
Caffarelli as if her life depended on it? She wasn't the
type of girl to have a fling. She didn't know how to be
casual about sex; she didn't *want* to be casual about it. It
went against everything she had learned over the years.

She pulled back out of his embrace, her gaze shifting away from his. 'I'm sorry...I'm not ready for this. I shouldn't have given you the impression I was...um... interested. I'm not normally so...so forward.'

'You don't have to apologise.'

She met his gaze again. 'You're not...angry?'

'Why would I be angry?'

'You said you wanted to make love...'

'I did. I do. But that doesn't mean I have to do so right this very minute. I might be pretty stubborn and determined in other areas of my life, but I would never force a woman to have sex with me against her will. It's not what a man with any decency does.'

Lily chewed at her lower lip, struck by how calm and in control he was. There was no sign of anger or resentment or any look that said 'how could you do this to me?'. No pushing or shoving, no gripping or grabbing and insisting on having his needs met.

Just respect and quiet calm.

Emotions she thought she had safely locked behind the do-not-open-again door in her mind suddenly sprang out of their confinement like a jack-in-the-box let loose. Tears she had sworn she would never shed again sprouted in her eyes. She choked back a sob and buried her head in her hands.

'Hey...' His gentle tone made her cry all the harder.

'I'm sorry.' She brushed at her streaming eyes with the back of her hand. 'You must think I'm a fool.'

'I don't think that at all.'

She took a shaky breath and tried to get her emotions back under control. 'You're the first man I've kissed in years. I never thought I'd ever want to get close to a man again. I deliberately didn't get close...until now.'

'You were…raped?' His tone was full of indignation, which she found strangely comforting.

'Yes.'

A muscle flicked in his jaw as if he was having trouble containing his outrage at the treatment she had been subjected to. 'Was the man arrested and charged?'

She shook her head. 'I didn't report it.'

His frown was so deep it created a V on his forehead. 'But what if he did it to some other girl?'

Lily crossed her arms over her body. 'I thought about that. A lot. But it was complicated.'

'That lowlife creep should be brought to justice. It's not too late. I can get you a good lawyer. It's not too late to file a charge. I know retrospective cases are much harder to prove but it would be worth it to have your day in court, even if it's only to name and shame him.'

'No, I don't want to do that. I *can't* do that.'

'Why can't you?' His frown was even more severe, his look even more forbidding. 'It's not right that he gets away with it. He hurt you, damn it. He should be made to pay for his crime. Do you have a good description of him? The police have face-recognition data files now. The technology is improving all the time. They might be able to track him on that to see if he's a serial offender.'

'He's not a serial offender.' Lily let out a long breath. 'Or at least, I don't think so. He was my best friend's older brother and he's got a law degree, along with his father, grandfather and great-grandfather.'

'You *know* him?'

'Most sex crimes are committed by people known to the victim. Random acts are still thankfully rare, although they do happen.' She knew she sounded like a police statement but she had heard the words so many times. 'I guess that's why I didn't take any precaution-ary steps. I didn't realise he was a threat until it was too late. Up until that night he'd been like a brother to me. But he was drunk and I was very tipsy. I thought we were just having a bit of a flirt with each other but suddenly everything changed. He got aggressive and before I knew it I was having unwanted sex. There was nothing I could do to stop it. He was very strong and I was under the influence of alcohol. I should have been more careful, but I guess everyone is wiser in hindsight.'

'You're blaming yourself for *his* lack of decency and control?' He gave her an incredulous look. 'How does that work? He should've realised you weren't able to give proper consent. It was his responsibility, not yours.'

Lily couldn't help a part-sad, part-wry smile. 'In spite of being known as a ruthless playboy, you're really a rather old-fashioned man, aren't you?'

His expression was dark and brooding. 'I'm not going to apologise for believing women deserve respect and protection.' He glanced at her arms. 'Is that why you started cutting?'

'Yes.'

'It's nothing to be ashamed of. The shame belongs to the man who took advantage of you. You were just try-ing to cope in the best way you could.'

'It wasn't a great way of coping.' She let out a ragged sigh. 'I wish I'd chosen something a little less perma-nent.'

'What, like drugs or alcohol or smoking? They're just other coping mechanisms, and they can have far more serious and dangerous implications in the long term.'

'I hate my scars.' Lily looked down at the white marks on her arms. 'I wish I could erase them.'

'Scars are a way of reminding ourselves of what we've learned in life. We all have them, Lily, it's just that some are more visible than others.'

Lily looked into his strong yet kind eyes and wondered yet again how his fiancée could have left him. He was such a noble man, so proud and yet so honourable. What woman wouldn't want to be loved and protected by such a man?

But then, he hadn't loved his fiancée, or so he had said. Was he capable of loving? Some men weren't. Neither were some women, and up until very recently she had been one of them.

Love?

You think you're in love with him?

Are you completely nuts?

Lily rubbed her hands over her shivering arms. 'I've been in the water too long.... I'd better go in. Do you need a hand getting out?'

'No, I might stay in for a while. Try some of that walking in water you suggested.'

'Is your cast still dry?'

'So far.'

Lily got out of the pool and turned to look at him. He hadn't moved at all. He was still watching her with a frown pulling at his brow. He looked so normal leaning there against the side of the pool. It was gut-wrenching to think his legs were not able to hold him upright. But maybe his limitations had given him the ability to understand hers. Or maybe he was just a truly wonderful man who didn't deserve what life had thrown his way. Either way she knew she would never forget this night. Being in his arms, feeling normal and desirable,

had touched her deeply. He had seen her scars and had
wanted her anyway.

He had made her feel beautiful and she hadn't felt
that in a very long time.

Raoul waited until Lily had gone back inside the château before he moved from the side of the pool. His insides were churning at what she had gone through. He
wanted to fix things for her, to seek justice, to undo the
wrong that had been done to her. It seemed so unfair
that she had suffered for so long on her own, hiding herself behind shapeless clothes, downplaying her features,
living half a life in order to avoid a repeat of what had
happened. The scars on her arms did nothing to detract
from her beauty, or at least not as far as he was concerned. He had always thought she was stunning, but
even more important to him was her inner beauty. She
was kind-hearted and gentle, compassionate yet spirited.

He felt deeply ashamed for thinking she had only
come for the money. How could he have misread her
so appallingly? She had wanted to leave at the first opportunity because she didn't feel safe. He had probably
terrified her with his snarly comments and black looks.
But, in spite of her fear, she had been drawn to him.

He thought of the way she kissed him, so unre-
strainedly, as if for those few moments she had acted
purely on instinct and allowed herself to be who she
was truly meant to be. What would it take to unlock
that frozen passion for good? To get her to come out of
her protective shell and live life the way it was meant
to be lived?

Was he the man to do it?

How could he help her when he couldn't even help

himself? He was stuck in a chair with legs that refused to work. He had nothing to offer her other than an affair to remember. He could just imagine her telling her friends about it some time in the future—the little fling she'd had with a guy in a wheelchair to get her confidence back. What a story that would be to dine out on.

He couldn't think of anything worse.

Why couldn't he have met her before his accident? They might have had a chance to build on the mutual attraction they felt. If he acted on it now, how could he be sure she wasn't feeling sorry for him? How could he know she wanted him for himself and not as a confidence boost?

Why did it matter? It had never mattered before. Sex was sex. It was a physical experience that didn't touch him emotionally. He'd had dozens of partners and he hadn't once thought of anything but the physicality of making love. It wasn't that he didn't like the women he'd slept with, although admittedly he had liked some more than others.

He wasn't comfortable with getting close to people emotionally. He had been very attached to his parents but the accident had taken them away from him and his brothers, shattering their lives in the blink of an eye. The family unit he had taken for granted had been destroyed. Everything that had been secure and sacred to them had been lost, even the very roof over their heads. The modest villa their mother had insisted they be brought up in to keep them grounded and in touch with those less fortunate than themselves had been sold within days of the funeral. They hadn't been consulted. Their grandfather had taken control and he'd had no time for tears or tantrums. He ruled with an iron fist and it came down on anyone who dared to thwart his will.

Raoul had shut down the feeling part of himself because it was safer to be distant and in control than to be up close and unguarded.

Turning it back on again was out of the question. Especially now....

CHAPTER TEN

DOMINIQUE WAS BEAMING from ear to ear when Lily came down for breakfast the next morning. 'You have worked a miracle, *oui*?'

'Yes, well, he's agreed to keep me on for the month, but I wouldn't get your hopes up too soon.'

'Not that.' Dominique pointed to the window. 'Look.'

Lily moved over to the bank of windows. Raoul was in his wheelchair down near the stables talking to Etienne who had one of the horses on a lead. It was a huge beast, strong and feisty-looking with a regally arched neck, wide nostrils and jittery stamping feet. But after a moment it quietened, stepped forward and nuzzled against Raoul's outstretched hand and then started rubbing its head against his chest with the sort of familiarity that spoke of deep affection and trust. Even from this distance she could see the smile on Raoul's face. A knotty lump came up in her throat and she had to swallow a couple of times to remove it.

'You are very good for him, Mademoiselle Archer.' Dominique's voice sounded like she had her own prickly lump to deal with. 'I did not think he would ever go outside again. It broke my heart to see him. He bred that stallion himself. People from all over the world pay a lot of money to have him sire their foals.'

'He looks gorgeous.'

Dominique gave her a cheeky look. 'I was talking about the horse.'

Lily felt a blush steal over her cheeks. 'So was I.'

The housekeeper poured Lily a coffee and handed it to her. 'Etienne told me you used to ride.'

'Not recently. I'd probably fall off as soon as the horse took a step.'

Dominique smiled at her. 'They say it is like riding a bike, no? You never forget.'

Lily took the cup and cradled in in both hands. 'Then I must be the exception to the rule because I've completely forgotten.'

'It's just a matter of confidence. The right time, the right horse, *oui*?'

'It's the most dangerous sport of all. It doesn't matter how well trained the horse is, they can still revert to their instincts.'

Dominique gave her a thoughtful look. 'Not all horses are like that.'

Lily put her cup down on the counter as she turned to leave. 'Maybe not, but all the ones I've met so far are.'

Raoul was already in the gym doing some weights when Lily came in an hour later. Although he didn't like admitting it, he felt better for having spent a bit of time outdoors. He had decided to relax his rule about going outside a bit further—just to the stables, not off the property or out in public. It went against every instinct he possessed to compromise, but last night in the pool had made him realise he could be short-changing himself not to stretch and push against every boundary that had been placed on him. It hadn't been easy getting down to the stables but Etienne had helped him down and back and the horses, particularly Mardi and his stallion, Firestorm, had appreciated his efforts.

'Etienne told me you are a former horsewoman.'

'Hardly that.'

'Would you be interested in exercising some of my horses while you are here?'

Her expression closed like a fist. 'No.'

'I have a very quiet mare that you—'

'You're not lifting that weight properly.' She picked up a lighter weight and demonstrated. 'See? You're incorporating the wrong muscles if you don't do it properly. It's a waste of time and effort if you don't do it the right way.'

Raoul didn't even look at the weight. 'What's wrong?'

'Nothing.'

'You're upset.'

She put the weight back down with unnecessary force, clanging it against the others on the rack. 'I'm here to help *you* rehabilitate. That's what you and your brother are paying me to do. I'm not here to get back in the saddle, either figuratively or literally.'

'I thought you might like some time off to relax. I don't expect you to spend all of your time here stuck indoors with me.' He scraped a hand through his hair and frowned. 'God knows it's bad enough for *me* being with me. I can't even imagine what it's like for you.'

There was a little silence.

'I don't find it hard being with you.' Her voice was so soft he almost didn't hear it.

Raoul looked at her. 'What, you enjoy my cutting sarcasm?'

'I think you push people away because you don't want them to see how much you're hurting.'

'Here we go.' He rolled his eyes. 'The psychology lecture. Have I paid for that or is that extra?'

Her chin came up a fraction. 'It's free.'

'Well, guess what? I don't want it. I was doing just fine until you came along.'

She folded her arms across her chest. 'Sure you were. That's why you were stuck inside this great, big old mausoleum with no one but your housekeeper to feed you meals through the tiny gap you allowed in the door. Oh, yes, you were getting on just fine and dandy.'

He glowered at her. 'And just how well are *you* getting on? Why don't you take a dose of your own therapy? Perhaps read your own aura for a change. See what everyone else sees when they look at you.'

She stiffened as if he had thrown something nasty at her; she was determined not to show how much it affected her. 'By "everyone else" I suppose you mean you?'

'What I see is completely different. I see a young woman who is deeply passionate but is too frightened to show it. I see how much you want to grab life with both hands, but those hands have been burnt once and you're too scared to reach for what you want because you don't want to get burnt again. What other people see is a distant, somewhat cold, frumpy woman—that's not who you are, Lily. You will never be happy until you are true to who you are meant to be.'

Her mouth flattened and her eyes flashed at him. 'I don't need you to sort out my life for me.'

'If you can't sort out your own, life what chance have you in sorting out mine?'

She opened and closed her mouth, her cheeks going a deep shade of pink as she turned away. 'I don't think this is going to work. I think it's best if I just leave.'

'You do that a lot, don't you?' Raoul said. 'You run away when things get uncomfortable. But avoiding a problem only means you won't be the one to eventually solve it.'

Every muscle in her back seemed to stiffen before she turned back to face him. 'And how are you going to solve *your* problems? By pushing everyone away who could help you? Good luck with that. I've tried that in the past and, believe me, it doesn't work.'

'Then let's both do it differently this time.' Raoul let out a long breath. 'Let's pretend my brother didn't engineer this. Let's just be two people who might be able to help each other get back on their feet...or back on the horse; whatever metaphor works.'

Her look was guarded. 'I'm not sure what you're suggesting.'

'Just be yourself. That's all I'm asking. I want to get to know the real Lily Archer.' He suddenly realised it was true. He wanted to know *everything* about her. He wanted to understand her and help her to claim back the life that had been stolen from her. She was a beautiful, warm-hearted girl who had been treated badly. She needed to regain her confidence and trust in people— and wasn't he the perfect man to do it?

Are you out of your mind? You can't help her. You can't even help yourself!

Raoul didn't want to listen to the voice of reason. This time he was going to go on his instincts rather than rationality. Spending time with her would make her feel more at ease with herself. Make her less shy, less defensive. It would be a two-way deal. She would be helping him to get back on his feet and he would help her embrace her life once more.

Her teeth sank into her bottom lip again. 'You might be disappointed.'

'I might be surprised. And you might be, too.' He gave her a crooked smile. 'I'm told I can be quite charming when I'm not snapping people's heads off.' He held out his hand. 'Truce?'

She put her small, soft hand in his. His almost swallowed it whole. 'Truce.'

Lily spent the next fortnight working with Raoul in the gym and on parallel bar exercises. She kept things as conservative as she could because she was concerned he was doing too much already. She had caught him a couple of times doing extra sessions in the gym, and she had seen him in the pool each afternoon since his plaster had come off, although she hadn't been brave enough to join him. It worried her that he was pushing himself beyond his body's capabilities. She didn't want to leave him worse off.

Leave him.

Those words made her uneasy every time she thought of them. She had to keep reminding herself that this was a job like any other. She wasn't supposed to get attached in any way to a client. She was supposed to do what she could to help them regain their mobility and strength and then move on to the next person who needed her. She wasn't supposed to daydream about their kisses or touches. She wasn't supposed to hope they would kiss her again or touch her other than incidentally.

He had kept a polite distance after that night in the pool. He had dined with her only a handful of times, mostly preferring to eat in his study while he worked. But she had seen the way his gaze kept homing in on her mouth now and again when he was speaking to her. It was like an involuntary impulse he couldn't control.

She wasn't much better. Only that morning she had helped him stabilise on the parallel bars and had come too close to him. He had momentarily lost his balance and she had stepped in to support him. She felt his warm, minty breath on her face and her heart had given a kick inside her chest in case he closed the small distance and covered her mouth with his.

But he hadn't.

His eyes had locked on hers for a heart-stopping moment. Her belly had flipped and then flopped. She had dropped her gaze to his mouth, instantly recalling how those firm lips and that searching, commanding tongue had wreaked such havoc with her own.

The seconds of silence had pulsed with sensual energy.

'That was a close one.' He gave her a wry smile as he rebalanced. 'I was about to fall flat on my face.'

'I wouldn't have let that happen.'

He looked at her for another long moment. 'Do you want to have dinner tonight?'

She arched a brow at him. 'You mean you don't have pressing paperwork or thousands of emails to see to?'

'Dominique told me you're lonely eating in the dining room all by yourself.'

'I'm not lonely.' Lily knew she had said it too quickly. It sounded far too defensive and prickly.

'I'll get Dominique to pack us a picnic.'

She blinked at him. 'A picnic?'

'You have something against picnics?'

'No, of course not. I love picnics. It's just I thought—'

'Meet me down by the lake. There's a glade on the western side. It'll be sheltered there if the wind picks up.'

'You don't want me to push you down there?'

He gave her a look. 'No.'

'But how will you—?'

'I have ways and means.'

The ways and means had four legs, a mane, a tail and looked terrifyingly skittish. Lily was waiting on a tartan blanket Dominique had packed along with the picnic when she saw Raoul coming towards her astride a glossy black stallion—she assumed it was the one she had seen him with before. He was leading another saddled horse on a rein and she recognised it as the gentle one called Mardi that Etienne had introduced her to that first day. Her heart gave a sudden lurch. What was he doing riding? How had he got on and what if he fell off? She sprang to her feet, almost tripping over the picnic basket as she did so. *'Are you out of your mind?'*

The stallion gave a snort and danced as if the ground beneath his hooves had suddenly turned to hot coals. Raoul kept his seat and soothed the horse in softly murmured French. The mare did nothing but look with considerable relish at the fresh baguette that was lying on the tablecloth. 'I thought you liked horses.'

'I do, but you're not supposed to be riding!'

'Why not?'

'Because you could fall off!'

'I won't fall off.' He stroked the stallion's satin-like neck. 'This is the perfect solution. I have four good legs instead of two bad ones.'

Lily gave him and the flighty horse a doubtful look. The stallion looked edgy and temperamental. Raoul was flirting with danger if he thought he could ride again as if nothing had changed. If he fell off he could damage his spine even more. The thought of him being injured further made her stomach curdle. Hadn't he had enough to deal with without looking for more tragedy?

'You're mad. You're asking for trouble. It's too soon. You could end up worse off. If you fall off and break both your legs, don't come running to me.' She blushed when she realised the absurdity of what she'd said. 'I meant that figuratively...of course.'

'Of course.' He grinned as he held out the mare's reins. 'Then supervise me. Come with me and make sure I'm being a good boy.'

She gave him a telling look. 'You and that stallion of yours are about as far away from good as it's possible to be.'

His eyes glinted at her. 'He looks mean and he acts mean, but he's a big softy underneath all that bluster.'

Lily took the mare's reins after a lengthy hesitation. The smell of leather and horse took her back to a time in her life when everything had been settled and in order. *Happy.* She stroked Mardi's shoulder as she prepared to mount. 'Good girl. Nice girl. Steady. Steady.' She managed to vault into the saddle without going over the other side like a circus clown, but it was a very near thing.

'You have a good seat.'

'Let's hope I keep it,' she muttered.

It didn't take her long to find her rhythm. The mare was as gentle and quiet as a lamb and her gait steady and sure. Raoul's stallion was anything but. He pranced and snorted but Raoul didn't appear to be having any trouble in keeping his seat. If anything he seemed to be enjoying himself. He looked relaxed and happy, his smile making him appear younger and more carefree than she had ever seen him. Looking at him now, no one would ever know he was unable to walk. He looked utterly gorgeous; fit, strong and devastatingly handsome.

He was the most wonderful, decent, honourable man she had ever met.

Hadn't the last two weeks confirmed that? He'd kept a polite distance, respecting her decision that night in the pool to refrain from committing to a physical relationship. He hadn't pressured her to talk about her past. He had simply given her the space to be herself.

He made her feel safe.

Her heart gave a little squeeze at the thought of going back to her life in London when this appointment was over.

Back to her female clients.

Back to her lonely nights watching something inane on television to fill in the hours until it was time to go to bed.

Back to reading books describing experiences she would never experience first-hand.

Like falling in love.

Lily gnawed at her lip. Maybe she wouldn't have to rely on books for that. Didn't she already feel a little bit in love with Raoul?

It was sheer and utter madness, of course. Deluded wishful thinking. Lunacy.

He wouldn't have looked twice at a girl like her if he hadn't been stuck with her at his château as a physical therapist. She had searched on her smart phone for a photograph of his ex-fiancée, Clarissa Moncrieff. Beautiful didn't even come close to describing the slim blonde woman with endless legs and a toothpaste-commercial smile. Looking at that photograph had made Lily feel like a small brown moth coming face-to-face with an exotic butterfly.

Sure, Raoul had kissed her a couple of times, but that didn't mean anything. Why would it? He'd kissed hundreds of women. He probably would have slept with her, too, if she'd given him the go ahead. He was used to having flings. Up until his relationship with Clarissa he hadn't spent more than six or eight weeks with the same partner. His interest in Lily had more to do with propinquity than anything else.

And she had better not forget it.

'Do you fancy a canter to the copse and back?' Raoul's voice pulled her out of her miserable mind wandering.

'Does Mardi have that particular gear?'

'If you give her plenty of encouragement.'

She gave the mare a gentle squeeze with her thighs and after a slow start the horse went from a trot to a lovely smooth canter. It was exhilarating to feel the breeze against her face as she rode towards the copse of trees. It brought back happy memories of a time in her life when things were hopeful and positive.

Raoul kept his stallion at a sedate pace but after a while he let him open out and stretch his legs. Lily watched as the horse's satin-clad muscles bunched and fired as he shot past. Raoul looked in his element, like a dark knight riding his finest steed.

He brought his horse to a standstill as he waited for her to catch up. 'All good?'

Lily couldn't keep the smile off her face. 'Wonderful.'

'You look beautiful when you smile.'

She *felt* beautiful when he looked at her like that. His eyes were meltingly dark and sexy as they held hers. She felt her stomach pitch when his gaze dropped down to her mouth. It never failed to stir her senses. It felt like a vicarious kiss each and every time.

'Are you hungry?' he asked.

'Starving.' Was he talking about food? *Was she?*

'But first I need to dismount.'

'How will you…?'

'Watch.' He made a clicking noise with his tongue and the stallion bent his forelegs to the ground. He eased himself out of the saddle and, using the horse as a prop, he came down on the picnic rug. For a fraction of a second it looked like he actually took all of his weight on his left leg. Lily was sure she hadn't imagined it, unless it was her wishful thinking back in overdrive. Had he been aware of doing it? He issued an order to the stallion in French and the horse moved away and started grazing as if butter wouldn't melt in his mouth.

'Wow, that is impressive. Has he always done that or did you just teach him?'

'I taught him ages ago. I just didn't realise how handy it would turn out to be.'

Lily could hear the strain of the last few weeks in his voice. Progress of any sort could be demoralising if it wasn't as fast and as perfect as one had hoped for. She had seen so many clients struggle with the emotional side of rehab. That final acceptance of limitation was the hardest thing to deal with. Some people never got there. They just couldn't cope with not being able to do the things they used to do. 'You're doing so well, Raoul. Did you realise you took your weight on your left leg just then? I'm sure I didn't imagine it.'

He gave her a grimace that fell short of being a smile. 'No, you didn't imagine it. I can stand for a few seconds, but I can't see myself walking into that church for my brother's wedding, can you?'

'The only thing that matters is your being there. I'm sure that's all your brother and his wife-to-be want.' Lily slipped out of the saddle and released the mare to graze alongside the stallion. 'You have to be there, Raoul. You don't really have a choice. You'll hurt Rafe and Poppy too much if you don't show up.'

He frowned as he picked a strand of grass and started toying with it. His right arm was still showing signs of the muscle wastage and topical dryness from being inside the cast and, though it was still swollen, his fingers were moving freely and seemingly without pain. 'I stood shoulder-to-shoulder with Rafe at our parents' funeral. It was the hardest thing I've ever had to do.' His frown deepened as if he had time-travelled to that dark, tragic time in his head. 'I put my feelings aside so I could support him. I swore on that day that I would always stand by him and Remy. That's what brothers are supposed to do. They support each other through everything and anything.'

'You don't have to physically stand by someone to support them. There are lots of ways to show you care about someone.' Like taking them on a picnic and arranging a quiet horse to ride so they get their lost confidence back.

Stop it. You're reading far too much into this.

His hazel eyes met hers. 'Rafe relies on me to back him up. Remy is like a loose cannon. I guess it's because we spoilt him so much. He was so young when our parents died. We tried to protect him and as a result he takes a hell of a lot for granted.'

'You did your best under terrible circumstances. No one could ask more of you than that.'

'I can't let Rafe down, but I can't bear the thought of only being half there.'

She reached for his left hand lying on the rug and squeezed it in her own. 'You won't be half there. *All* of you will be there. Can't you see that? You are much more than your physical self. Much, *much* more.'

He picked up her hand and brought it to rest against his chin. She felt the prickle of his stubble against her fingers and a wave of longing rolled through her as his eyes meshed with hers. 'I wish I'd met you before my accident.'

Her heart gave a sudden kick against her ribcage. 'Why?'

'I think I could've fallen in love with you.'

Like you have a choice?

'What's stopping you now?' She could not believe she'd just asked that! What was she doing, asking for a slap down? Hadn't her self-esteem taken enough hits? Why would he fall in love with her?

She was a nondescript brown moth, not a beautiful butterfly.

His fingers moved against hers. They seemed to be relaying a message that was at odds with his words. 'Reason. Rationality. Responsibility.'

'The three Rs.'

'You've been reading about me and my brothers.'

Lily decided there was no point pretending she hadn't. 'Rakes. Rich. Ruthless. Everyone's been calling you and your brothers that for years.'

He frowned as he looked at her fingers encased in his own. 'We're one down on the rakes. Two, if you count me.'

Lily wondered if he was thinking of his ex. Even if he hadn't loved Clarissa he must surely be missing the sex. He was an intensely physical man. Virile. Potent. *Irresistible.*

He brought his eyes back to hers and her belly did a complicated gymnastics manoeuvre. 'Do you realise this is the longest period I've been celibate?'

'Wow, must be some sort of record, huh? What is it, six or seven weeks?' Her face was hot. It felt like it was on fire.

You're discussing his sex life?
What is wrong with you?

He gave her a grim smile. 'Nine.'

'Wow. That's a long time. It's like a decade for someone like you, right? Maybe more like a century. Or a millennium.' *Shut up!*

His thumb traced a lazy circle over the back of her hand. 'I guess it's been even longer for you.'

Lily looked down at their joined hands. Her hand was so small compared to his. Her skin so light. It was like a physical embodiment of everything that was different about the worlds they came from.

Hers was plain and boring.

His was colourful and exciting.

The silence ballooned until it seemed to suck all the oxygen out of the air.

'Have you...?'

'I haven't.'

They had spoken at exactly the same time.

'You go first,' Raoul said.

Lily blushed and looked down again at her hand within his. 'I haven't got back on the horse, so to speak. It wasn't that I was all that good at it to start with. I'd had a couple of relationships but I can't say I ever felt that certain spark everyone talks about.' *Like the one she could feel now as his thumb did another circle on her hand.* 'I guess I'm not a very passionate person. As a sexual partner, I'm what you'd call vanilla, not rocky road.'

His eyes went to her mouth. 'I hate rocky road. Vanilla is simple and uncomplicated. Understated. Elegant. And it's a perfect blend with other flavours. It goes with just about anything.'

Were they still talking about ice-cream?

Lily willed him to look at her. Couldn't he see how much she wanted him? Her body was humming with need. It was a wonder he couldn't hear it. It was like a roaring sound inside her ears.

Her blood was racing with it.

Firing with it.

Heating with it.

Exploding with it.

She wanted him.

It was a powerful, overwhelming feeling that was at odds with everything she had previously clung to. Pride, safety and security were nothing when it came down to the wire.

She wanted to feel like a woman. She wanted to be *his* woman.

He looked at her and the universe seemed to take a breath and hold it.

Lily saw the heat and the longing. She saw the need and desperation she felt in her body reflected in his gaze. She reached for him as he reached for her.

'I want you.' They said it in unison.

'Are you sure?' he said.

She stroked his stubbly jaw, mesmerised by the way his gaze had softened. 'I've never been surer. I want this. I want you. I don't want my bad memories to haunt me any more. Give me good ones to replace them.'

To store away and revisit when this is all over, as it surely will be all too soon.

He cupped her face in with his hands, his gaze dark, concerned. Conflicted. 'I'm not the right man for you. I'm not the right man for any woman right now.'

Lily gazed into his warm green-brown eyes. 'I think you're the perfect man. It will be like the first time for both of us.'

'I can't offer you anything but this.' His mouth was already nudging hers, his breath mingling with hers in that hotly intimate way that made her shiver and shudder with desire. 'You have to understand and accept that.'

'This is all I want.' *Liar. You want the whole she-bang. You want the fairytale you keep reading about: boy meets girl, boy loves girl, boy rides with girl off into the sunset.* 'I want to feel passion again. I want to feel alive again.'

'I want that, too.' His voice sounded deep and tortured. 'You have no idea of how much I want that.'

'Show me.' She breathed the words against his lips. 'Show me...please?'

CHAPTER ELEVEN

RAOUL HAD BEEN making love—having sex was probably a more accurate way of putting it—with women since he was seventeen. He knew their bodies. He knew what turned them off and what turned them on. He was a master at seduction. He knew every move, every caress, every touch and stroke that would make his partner feel as if he was the most amazingly competent lover in the world.

But with Lily Archer he felt like he was starting all over again. He didn't have a clue. He felt out of his depth. He was floundering. Worried. Terrified he might hurt her or make her scared.

Her mouth felt like soft velvet under his. It was so responsive, hungry, searching and yet hesitant, as if she were still feeling her way with him. Relearning the steps, tasting, touching and feeling. Her shyness mixed with her simmering passion made his body throb and ache with need. The way she touched him, the way her arms came around his neck, the way her fingers threaded through his hair made his desire for her roar inside his loins.

She made little murmuring sounds of pleasure as he explored her mouth. But he had to keep a firm lid on his response. He was fully erect and aching to let go but she was nowhere near ready for him. He sensed it in the subtle ways she moved, jerking back, shifting, like a shying horse facing a jump that was too high.

'I'm not going to hurt you.' He stroked a finger down the curve of her cheek. 'Trust me, Lily.'

She gave him a tentative smile that was little more than a tiny flutter of her lips. 'I trust you.'

'If you want to stop at any point, then you just have to tell me.'

'I don't want you to stop.' She moved her pelvis against his. It was a subtle movement, probably more instinctive than conscious, but it caused a raging inferno to roar through his veins. 'I want you to make love to me.'

He moved a gentle hand over her breast. It fitted his palm perfectly, her nipple pressing against his flesh as if in search of his touch. He wanted to feel her skin on skin, to feel her silky heat against his, to feel the satin of her flesh against the rough rasp of his.

He slid a hand under her top, gauging her reaction, letting her dictate the terms, but if anything she encouraged his exploration. She arched her spine like a cat so her breasts would be in closer contact with his hands.

He lowered his mouth to the tight pink nubs of her nipples he'd exposed, savouring each one in turn. She bucked and writhed as he tantalised her senses, her hands grasping his head, her fingers digging into his scalp as he rolled his tongue over and around her sensitive flesh.

She suddenly eased back from him. 'Should I get, um, undressed?'

She looked so adorably out of her depth. He was used to women shrugging their clothes off before he got them through the door. He was used to women showing off their assets in clinging, revealing clothing that left nothing to the imagination. He was used to women telling him what they wanted and going out to get it, no holds barred.

Touch here. This hard. This slow; this fast.

It was so damned mechanical.

Lily Archer looked up at him with those big dark blue eyes and made him feel…like a man.

'I think that's my job.' His voice sounded like a croak. His hands felt like a fumbling teenager's on his first date. He peeled away her top, revealing her slim chest, small, pert breasts and her amazing abs and his breath stalled in his throat. 'Wow.'

She gave him a sheepish look. 'They look bigger when I'm wearing a push-up bra. It's sort of like false advertising.'

Raoul smiled as he laid a hand on the flat plane of her abdomen. 'Your breasts are beautiful.'

She shuddered under his touch. 'I like your hands. They're…gentle.'

'I like your body.' He stroked his hand down the length of her cotton-trouser-clad thigh.

Her gaze fell away from his. 'It's ugly.'

He pushed her chin up so her eyes met his again. 'It's not ugly. It's who you are now. You can't change it even if you wanted to.'

She gave him a frustrated, anguished look. 'I don't want to be like this. I wish I could get rid of my scars. It's not who I am now. I want to move on. I hate that I have this mark of who I was back then permanently etched on my body like a tattoo. I'm not that girl any more. I just got lost for a while and I've had to pay for it ever since.'

Raoul knew exactly what she was feeling. He wanted to move on, too. He didn't want to be trapped in his body, in a body that didn't represent him as a person, as a man. But what other choice did he have? What choice did she have? They were both trapped.

He brushed back her hair from her forehead. 'Do you think I want to live in my body the way it is? I lie awake at night terrified that this might be as good as it ever gets. You have some scars. I know that's hard to deal with, but they're only as permanent as you allow them to be.'

Wasn't there something in that he should be taking on board?

'I want to be normal.'

'You *are* normal.' His body registered just how normal by the way it was responding to hers. Hard, urgent, desperate.

She traced a fingertip over his bottom lip. 'Make me feel normal. Make me forget about anything but what's here and now.'

What was here and now was how wonderful, how magical her mouth felt beneath his. He gathered her close, delighting in the feel of her moulding herself to him as if she had been looking for him all of her life. There were no awkward shifts or adjustments. She moved into him like a key fitting into a tricky lock.

It felt so good to have her that close. Close enough to feel the contours of her body against his. He felt a sense of rightness that he had never felt before.

He tried to push the thought aside but it kept coming back, niggling at him, jostling him, urging him like an obsessed terrier dropping a tennis ball at its handler's feet.

He wanted this feeling to last.

Lily felt his hands moving over her so tenderly, so carefully. He was taking his time, peeling away her clothes piece by piece, kissing each part of her he exposed in warm, soft-as-air caresses that made her spine tingle like bubbles in a glass. He kissed each and every scar on her arms, his mouth and lips spreading a pathway of heat through her body.

He helped her get out of her cotton trousers, his mouth moving down her stomach, his tongue taking a little dip in the tiny pool of her belly button before coming to the top of her knickers.

She stiffened, her stomach churning. Was he thinking how awful the tops of her legs looked compared to his ex-fiancée's? She bet Clarissa Moncrieff's gorgeous long cellulite-free legs didn't have a single blemish on them. She bet his ex had waxed and exfoliated and spray-tanned regularly. Was he thinking how plain and sensible Lily's chain-store underwear was? Any moment now he would pull back in revulsion, make some excuse that this couldn't continue. Oh, God! Why had she asked him to make love to her? It was so desperate and gauche of her.

'Hey, hey, hey.' His voice was a soft, deep, soothing rumble, his hand gentle and steadying as it came to rest on her stomach. 'You're beautiful. I mean it, Lily. So very natural and beautiful.'

Her breath caught in her chest as he began stroking her thighs in long, smooth gentle caresses that made her tense muscles slowly relax. She stopped breathing altogether when he put his mouth to her left thigh, his lips moving over her scarred flesh like the brush of a teasing feather.

He did the same to her right thigh, moving tantalisingly close to the moist, swollen, pulsing heart of her. 'I want... I want...' She didn't know how to ask for the release she craved. She had never felt the need building quite like this before. It was rising to a crescendo in her body, every nerve tensing and twitching in feverish anticipation.

He stroked a lazy finger down the cotton-covered seam of her body. Close but not close enough. She gave a little whimper and arched her spine. 'I want *you.*'

He peeled away her knickers and traced her seam again. It made her gasp to feel the thickness of his finger against her moist heat. He brought his mouth to her, gently tasting her essence, teasing her until she was grasping his head like a drowning person with a rescuer. The sensations started as a ripple and then came smashing over her in a series of waves. She cried out in a breathless, gasping sobs, shaken to the core of her being by the out-of-control passion—not someone else's, but her own.

'You're very good at this.' *Did she sound unsophisticated?*

He gave her a smouldering smile. 'So are you.'

Lily shyly stroked a hand over his chest. Somehow while he had been kissing her she had managed to undo his shirt buttons but he was still fully clothed. Had he done that deliberately, to stop her from being overwhelmed by seeing his naked body? 'I want to touch you...'

He covered her hand with one of his. 'It might have to wait for some other time.'

Some other time?

Her stomach did that butter-churn thing again. He didn't want to make love to her? Was she so hideous?

But *surely* he wanted her? She'd felt his erection. She could *still* feel it pressing against her right thigh.

He doesn't want you. He wants his ex. His beautiful, perfect ex.

Lily slipped her hand out from under his and started to hunt for her clothes. 'Right; well, then. I wouldn't want to force you or anything. God, no; that would be ridiculously ironic, don't you think?'

'I don't have a condom.'

She stopped wrestling herself back into her trousers to look at him. 'Oh…'

He gave her a rueful look. 'I don't think Dominique would have packed one in the picnic basket, do you?'

She arched her brows cynically. 'I don't know. I'm sure if you'd asked her to she would have.'

He frowned at her. 'You think that's why I set up this picnic?'

'It was a way of riding two horses with one jockey, so to speak. You got me back in the saddle—both of them.'

'You've got it all wrong, Lily.' He raked a hand through his hair, making it look even more tousled. 'I didn't have any intention of sleeping with you.'

'You didn't sleep with me.' She threw him a flinty look. 'You *serviced* me.'

His mouth went into a tense line. 'If you think I'm the sort of man who would have sex with a vulnerable young woman without using a condom then you're even more—'

'What?' she flashed back before he could finish his sentence. 'Screwed up? Nutty? Crazy?'

His jaw moved in an out as if he was trying to control his temper. 'Stop putting words in my mouth.'

'It's what you're thinking, isn't it?' She stuffed her feet back in her shoes. 'It's what everyone thinks when they see my legs and arms.' She sent him another fiery glare. 'And, just for the record, I am *not* vulnerable.'

'Yes, you are. You're vulnerable and scared and you won't let anyone get close enough to help you.'

'You're a fine one to talk,' she threw back.

'I let *you* in, didn't I?'

'Grudgingly.'

There was a short, tense silence.

'You have helped me, Lily. You've helped me a lot.'

Lily felt her anger dissipating at his gruff tone. 'I have?'

'I think you're right about Rafe's wedding.' His mouth twisted resignedly. 'I need to be there, chair or no chair.'

She felt a wave of unexpected emotion swamp her. She blinked a couple of times to stop the tears that were threatening to spill. If nothing else, she had achieved what his brother had paid her for. Raoul was going to go to the wedding. It would be a big step for him to be out in public but it was an important one. 'I'm so glad, for you, for Rafe and Poppy.'

'Will you come with me?'

'I don't think it's my place to barge in on a—'

'I want you there.' His tone had a thread of steel to it. 'You're my physical therapist. I might need you to massage a tight muscle or stroke my ego or something.'

'Your *ego*?'

'Will you do it?'

She caught the inside of her mouth with her teeth. A family wedding. It was so…so *personal*. She would have to witness other people experiencing what she most desperately wanted for herself: love, commitment and a happy future. 'I don't know....'

'It's another ten days away. You have plenty of time to make up your mind.'

Lily wondered if he were asking her to accompany him for other reasons. It would be a very public gathering. There would be press everywhere. No doubt there would be speculation about his broken engagement. Was he looking for a way to divert public attention, having her pose as his stand-in date? 'I have to go back to London straight after. I have clients booked in. There's a waiting list.'

'I won't keep you longer than the month. After the wedding, you are free to leave.'

His words made her heart suddenly contract. He hadn't wanted her here in the first place. Why was she disappointed he was already planning for her departure?

'OK. Fine. Good.'

'We should do something about this food Dominique has prepared,' he said. 'She might not have packed condoms, but there is just about everything else inside this pack.'

Lily sat down on the blanket beside him. She couldn't think of a time when she had felt less like eating. She made a token effort but later she couldn't recall what she ate. The conversation was stilted. Awkward. She sensed Raoul couldn't wait for the evening to be over. Even the horses seemed to pick up on the restless mood. They twitched their tails and pricked their ears at the slightest sound.

Finally it was time to leave.

She made an attempt to pack up the picnic basket

but Raoul intercepted her. 'Leave it. Etienne will take it back to the château later.'

'Do you need a hand to get back on your—?'

He cut her off with a look. 'I'll be fine. Take Mardi back to the stables. One of the other stable hands will unsaddle her for you. I'll wait here for Etienne.'

Raoul was drowning. The water was over his head. His limbs were dead. His lungs were exploding. He thrashed against the restraint of the water but it didn't feel like water. It felt like fabric. He punched it away and he heard a choked-off cry.

He froze.

Woke up. Blinked. Realised he was in his bedroom and that Lily was sitting on the edge of his bed clutching her chin, her eyes as wide as dinner plates. 'Did I hurt you?' His insides turned to gravy. 'Tell me I didn't hurt you.'

'You didn't.' She dropped her hand from her face. 'Not really.'

He could see the red mark where his hand had glanced against her chin. He touched it gently with his finger. 'I'm sorry. I sometimes have terrible nightmares. I should've warned you.'

'I heard you shouting.'

Somehow his finger had gone from her chin to the soft pillow of her lower lip. 'Did I wake you?'

'I wasn't asleep.'

His gaze locked on hers. She looked so young and so...so unpretentious. Unprepared. Natural. Her hair was free about her shoulders. It smelt of honeysuckle and jasmine, familiar, homely yet exotic. He traced her top lip and then her bottom lip with his finger. 'Why weren't you able to sleep?'

Her eyes fell away from his. 'Just one of those nights, I guess...'

'I was having one of those myself.'

Her eyes came back to his. 'Can I get you a drink or something? Milk? Hot chocolate? Cocoa?'

'No.' He moved his thumb over her lip again. 'Thanks.'

Her lips shifted in an uncertain-looking on-off smile. 'I guess I should let you get back to bed...'

'Stay.'

She blinked a couple of times. 'Stay?'

'Talk to me. Keep me company. Distract me.'

She rolled her lips together. 'I don't think that's part of my job description...'

'I don't want you to stay here as my physical therapist.' He held her gaze with his. 'Stay for another reason.'

The tip of her tongue made a nervous dart out over her lips. 'What other reason could there be?'

He brought her closer, his mouth coming down to within a breath of hers. 'Think of one.' And then he covered her mouth with his.

It was a very good reason. The best *possible* reason. Lily couldn't think of any better reason to be in his bedroom and in his arms being kissed so soundly other than that it was exactly where she wanted to be.

His arms gathered her close to his body, his mouth moving on hers with devastatingly erotic expertise. His tongue slid into her mouth, stroking against hers, teasing it into duelling with his. Her belly flipped like a pancake as he deepened the kiss even further.

He pressed her backwards on the bed, his weight supported by his elbows, his lips and tongue working their magic on hers. 'You taste so damn good,' he groaned against her mouth.

Lily kissed him back with all the passion that had been ignited that evening of the picnic. It had been ignited from the first moment she had met him—that instant spark of attraction, that magnetic pull, that irresistible lure of polar opposites.

The need she felt for him was a throbbing ache that pulsed between her legs. She had never been more aware of her body. He had awakened the dormant sensations, making them explode like fireworks in front of a raw flame.

His hands moved over her, shaping her breasts, touching her, tantalising her with the promise of more. Her nipples were tight and sensitive, her flesh hungry for the hot, wet swirl of his tongue and the sexy graze of his teeth.

She gave a gasp as he pushed up her pyjama top, his hands warm and sure on her body. She shivered as his mouth closed over her nipple, the sucking motion making every hair on her head lift up at the roots. He was gentle yet determined, drawing from her a response she had not thought she was capable of giving. Her body writhed beneath his, looking for more connection, for flesh on flesh, for satiation.

'I don't want to rush you,' he said.

'You're not rushing me.' She kissed him, once, twice, three times. 'I want this. I want you.'

He smiled against her lips. 'At least this time I'm a bit better prepared.'

'Down at the lake… I thought you didn't want me.'

He pulled back to look down at her. 'How could you possibly think that?'

Lily looked at a point of stubble on his chin rather than meet his eyes. 'I thought it must be because of my scars. I guess I'm not used to men who are responsible enough to stop and think about using protection.'

He tipped up her chin. 'Not all men are irresponsible and selfish, *ma petite*. And you should stop worrying about your scars. They don't define you as a person. It's your behaviour, not your appearance, that does that.'

She touched his bottom lip with her fingertip. 'You've always dated such exquisitely beautiful women.'

'Some of the most beautiful women I've been with have also been the most boring. You, on the other hand, are captivating, intriguing and utterly irresistible.' He brought his mouth back to hers, pressing a lingering kiss to her lips until she forgot about her insecurities and thought of nothing but how he made her feel.

He made her feel good. Alive.

On fire.

Lily touched his chest, sliding her hands down over his taut abdomen shyly, hesitantly. She felt him suck in a breath as her hand came to the top of his groin. She felt the smooth head of his erection bump against her hand and a tight fist of intense longing grabbed at her insides.

She couldn't stop herself from exploring him. He was so thick and full, so strong yet contained. She had never really thought of a man's body as beautiful before, or at least not this part of a man's body. She ran her fingertip over the moist tip of his penis, that most primal signal of readiness. She felt her own intimate moisture; it was a silky reminder that she was just as aroused as he was. 'I want you inside me...'

'I want to be inside you.'

She shivered in anticipation as he reached for a condom. He came back over her, his weight balanced on his arms, his legs a sexy tangle with hers. He gently eased her thighs apart, hooking one leg over his hip as his mouth came back to hers.

She felt the probe of his body against her. It was subtle and yet urgent. She moved against him, silently giving him permission, wanting him so badly her body was aching with it.

'I'll take it slowly.' His words were a sexy rumble against her lips.

She arched her spine again, searching for his possession. She didn't want him slow. She wanted him fast. She wanted him to feel the same pressing need she felt building in her body.

He gave a guttural groan and slid partway inside, waiting for her to accommodate him. 'Are you OK?'

'I want *all* of you.' She dug her hands into his buttocks, urging him on. *'Now.'*

He went in a little deeper, still keeping control. 'It will be much better for you, the longer I prepare you.'

'I'm prepared.' She pressed her mouth to his, feeding off him hungrily while her inner muscles gripped him tightly. *I'm so prepared!*

He thrust deeper, his face burying against her neck as he fought for control. She caught his rhythm, feeling every movement, her senses going off into a tailspin when his fingers came into the action, caressing her intimately to trigger that final cataclysmic release.

She shattered into a million pieces, her body shaking and shuddering with an explosive orgasm that left her spent and limp in his arms.

'Good?'

She could barely speak. 'Wow...'

He brushed her hair back from her face, his look surprisingly tender. 'You did it.'

She pointed a finger at his chest. '*You* did it.'

'It takes two to tango, as they say. We *both* did it.'

'Not quite.' Lily used her inner muscles to squeeze him. 'You haven't...'

'I'm about to.'

She felt a shiver race down her spine at the smouldering look in his eyes. She felt him start to move again, the slow but steady build-up of thrusts that made her flesh tingle all over again. She didn't think it was possible for her body to experience another orgasm so soon after the previous one but within seconds she was flying away again. She clung to him as he buried his face into her neck as he pumped his way into oblivion.

It was a long moment before he moved away from her.

He had a little frown on his face as he disposed of the condom. He sat on the edge of the bed, his back turned to her. Lily wondered with a painful pang if he was thinking of his ex. How many times had they made love? How long had they been together? Was he comparing Lily's response to hers?

'I guess I should go back to my room.' She gave him a self-deprecating look when he turned to look at her. 'I'm not sure I want Dominique to find me slinking out of your bedroom first thing in the morning.'

'Don't go.'

She rolled her lips together, not sure what to make of his unfathomable expression. 'You want me to stay with you all night?'

A tiny muscle flicked in his jaw. 'Not just tonight. Every night until you go back to London.'

He was offering her a relationship. An affair. A temporary one.

Very temporary.

'Obviously I'm very flattered, but—'

'But you want more.' It was a statement not a question. 'The thing is, Lily, this is all I'm capable of right now.'

Would she sound terribly gauche, asking for more? What chance was there that a man like him would fall in love with someone like her?

Men like Raoul Caffarelli did not fall in love with shy plain Jane English girls with scars.

It just showed how hopelessly romantic she was. But a short affair was all he was going to offer her because he would not commit to anything else unless he was fully mobile. That was the sort of man he was. He could not envisage a future any other way. Could she risk her heart for a hope that might never come to fruition? He had undoubtedly improved in the last fortnight but that was no guarantee that he would regain his full mobility.

He was twice, *four* times the man of some of the able-bodied ones she'd met. He had so much to offer. He was not the least bit diminished by his physical limitations.

Why couldn't he see that?

Because he was so damned uncompromising and stubborn, that was why. He thought in terms of black or white, either-or. There were no shades of in between.

What if she said yes? It would give her a little under two weeks of memories that were certainly a whole lot better than the ones she had come with.

He was a passionate and skilled lover. He was a good

man, a decent, lovely man to be around. He was respect-
ful and kind. Considerate.

And she was in love with him.

Which was why she should say no. Right now. Nip it
in the bud. *Do not pass Go. Do not take another step.
Do not stomp in where angels fear to tread.*

'I'll stay.'

CHAPTER TWELVE

'So HOW ARE things going with Miss Archer?' Rafe asked when he phoned a few days later.

'Fine.'

'Just "fine"?'

'Good.'

'So you're talking to her, then?'

Raoul didn't want to go into the details of his current relationship with Lily. He hadn't quite got his own head around it. All he knew was he enjoyed being with her. She was easy company, gentle and kind, caring. He enjoyed watching her wake up each morning, rub her sleepy eyes and give him that shy smile of hers. He loved the feel of her body nestled up against his when she slept.

He loved *watching* her sleep.

She looked like Sleeping Beauty, so pale and so beautiful. He loved the way she responded to him so passionately. She was far more confident now as a lover. He had never been with a partner who surprised and delighted him as much as she did. It was like discovering sensuality all over again. He was aware of his body in ways he had never been before. Her touch was like magic. He was sure it was one of the reasons he had improved his mobility.

He *felt* stronger.

'You *are* talking to her, aren't you?' Rafe's voice jolted him back to the moment.

'Of course I'm talking to her. So...how're the wedding plans going?'

'Whoa, quick subject change. What's going on?'

'Nothing.' Raoul gave himself a mental kick for answering too quickly. It was hard to pull the wool over Rafe's eyes, even over the phone. 'Nothing's going on.'

'You're not sleeping with the hired help, are you?'

He felt his back come up. 'Lily is not the hired help. She's—'

'So it's *Lily* now.' Rafe gave an amused little chuckle. 'I must say I didn't see that coming. I didn't think she was your type. Not compared to—'

'Shut the hell up.'

'You're not still cut up about that bimbo dumping you, are you? Come on, Raoul. She's not worth it. At your age you should be looking for love, not looks.'

Raoul clenched his jaw. 'I'm not interested in falling in love.'

'Famous last words.' Rafe chuckled again. 'I said them myself and look what happened—I fell hook, line, and sinker for Poppy and I couldn't be happier. I can't believe that this time next week we'll be man and wife.'

'Look, I'm happy for you. I really am. Just don't go expecting me to follow you down the aisle any time soon. Pick on Remy. He's the one who needs to settle down.'

'Has he been to see you? Called you? Texted? Emailed?'

'He came the day before you brought Lil...Miss Archer. I haven't heard from him since. Why, what's he up to?'

'I don't know.' A thread of concern seemed to underpin Rafe's voice. 'I think he's having some sort of showdown with Henri Marchand over one of his major holdings or properties. I've heard on the grapevine that Marchand is desperate for funds. He made a couple of investments that didn't pay off.'

'Karma.'

'You could be right.' Rafe let out a breath. 'I just hope Remy knows what he's doing. He's juggling a lot of finance just now. He's been trying to buy into the Mappleton hotel chain, as well. He's been working on the negotiations for months. If he pulls it off it would be the biggest coup of all of our careers. But apparently Robert Mappleton is ultra-conservative. Word has it he refuses to do business with Remy because he thinks Remy's too much of a playboy.'

'I can't see Remy marrying someone just to nail a deal, can you?' Raoul's tone was dry.

Rafe gave a laugh. 'Speaking of weddings… Are you coming to mine?'

'Wild horses couldn't keep me away.'

Lily was in the garden picking flowers for the table when Raoul came out to her. He was in his manual chair but he had been up on his feet for at least a minute during their gym session earlier. He had taken three steps—four, if you counted the one before he had to grasp the rails. It was an enormous leap forward. It was still too early to say whether he would continue to improve, but she was cautiously optimistic.

He looked tired now, however. He had lines of strain around his mouth. She knew he still had a lot of pain but he refused to take any medication. She knew he didn't sleep properly. She had woken so many times to find him watching her with a frown on his face. Was it pain that put that frown there, or was it because she wasn't the woman he had thought would be sharing his bed?

'Did you want me?'

He gave her a sexily slanted smile. 'Always.'

Always? He wasn't offering always. He had offered her here and now. And here and now would be over in days. She had resigned herself to it. She would be going home and that would be it. She wouldn't see him again.

Her heart gave a painfully tight squeeze.

Ever.

'Dominique knows.'

'That I want you?'

'That you've *had* me.' She gave him a see-what-you've-done look. 'I tried to deny it, but my bed hasn't been slept in for over a week, so it wasn't like I could convince her otherwise.'

'And that bothers you?'

'Of course it bothers me. I'm not some scullery maid slipping upstairs for a bit of slap and tickle with the lord of the manor. I feel...awkward. Embarrassed. Ashamed.'

'Why?'

She tossed the roses she'd gathered into the basket she was holding. 'Dominique thinks it's all going to end up like some sort of fairytale. I think you should talk to her. Tell her how it is.'

His mouth tightened. 'I don't need to explain myself to my domestic staff.'

Explain it to me, then. Tell me *where I stand.*

'Fine.' She snapped another rose off and dropped it in the basket. 'But I'm not coming to the wedding with you. I think that's taking things way too far.'

'I want you with me.'

'Why?' She felt her heart contract again. 'So you can show everyone you've moved on from Clarissa?'

'It has *nothing* to do with Clarissa.'

'It has everything to do with her. You're not ready for a relationship.'

His jaw went down like a clamp.

'I've already made the arrangements. You can't *not* come.'

'I haven't got anything to wear.'

'I've got that covered.'

'You bought me clothes?' Lily glared at him. 'Is that what you did? *How could you?* How could you make me feel like some sort of tawdry kept mistress?'

His eyes hardened like diamonds. 'You're not my mistress.'

'No, of course not.' She gave him a testy look. 'I'm just your physical therapist with benefits.'

His mouth was pulled so tight it looked white around the edges. 'I don't want to have this conversation now.'

'Fine.' She tossed her head and went in hunt of another rose to pick. 'Don't have it, then.'

He blew out an audible breath. 'What is wrong with you? Why are you being so…so antagonistic all of a sudden? You knew how it was going to be. I didn't make any promises to you.'

Lily put the rose in her basket. The velvet petals and the savage thorns were a poignant reminder of what love was like: beautiful but excruciatingly painful.

No, he hadn't made any promises.

She was the one with the serious case of wishful thinking. A couple of times she'd caught him watching her when he had thought she was still asleep. He'd had a look of such tenderness and longing in his eyes it had made her wonder if he would open his heart to her. She was wrong. Clearly. 'No, that's right. You didn't.'

'Let's not fight now, Lily.' His jaw was set in an uncompromising line. 'Please…' His voice lost its harsh edge, showing a tiny glimpse of how vulnerable he was feeling, 'Not now.'

Lily felt herself caving in. What was she doing ruining their last few hours arguing with him? He had made up his mind.

She had better get used to it.

The Oxfordshire church was full of fragrant flowers. Raoul had to steel himself as he wheeled up the aisle. It reminded him of his parents' funeral. The cloying scent was overpowering. Sickening. Thank God there wasn't a choir.

He caught a glimpse of Lily sitting in one of the pews. She gave him a shy smile that tugged on his heart like stitches being pulled. She was wearing the designer outfit he had bought her. He couldn't make up his mind whether it suited her or not. Personally, he preferred her without clothes, but that was just his opinion. The slim-fitting, shell-pink suit clung to her neat figure like a glove. Her hair was swept up in an elegant twist on top of her head and she had put on a modest amount of make-up that highlighted her creamy complexion, regally high cheekbones and the deep blue of her eyes.

Rafe was standing at the altar, looking dashing if not a little nervous. Remy hadn't yet arrived, and no one was entirely sure if he would, but that was Remy for you.

'How're you doing?' Rafe asked as Raoul parked his chair alongside.

'I think that's supposed to be my line.'

'You made it.'

'I made it.'

Rafe swallowed a couple of times and then turned to face the front of the church. 'I feel a bit nervous.'

'I can tell.'

Rafe glanced at him. 'You can?'

'You keep tugging at your left sleeve. Dead giveaway.'

'Got that.'

Remy suddenly appeared at the portal of the church and did a last-minute adjustment to his bow tie as he ambled down the aisle. 'Were you guys waiting for me?'

Rafe gave him a look. 'Glad you could make it.'

Remy gave one of his renowned charming grins. 'Hey, Raoul, you're looking good. Walking yet?'

Raoul stretched his mouth into a rictus smile. 'Almost.'

The organist began playing. The beautiful cadences of Pachelbel's *Canon in D* swelled to the rafters.

'Here comes the bride....' Rafe's voice sounded hoarse with emotion.

Raoul looked at Poppy as she floated up the aisle. She only had eyes for his brother. Her face was glowing with love, with absolute rapture. He felt a pain in the middle of his chest. Would he ever see a bride come towards him with the same depth of love?

'Dearly beloved, we are gathered together...'

The sacred vows were a form of torture. To have and to hold. For richer for poorer...

In sickness and in health.

Did his brother realise what the hell he was promising? Did Poppy? There was only so much sickness a relationship could endure. It was too much to ask someone to stick by you no matter what. Life could throw some horrible curve balls. He had caught one fair in the middle of his gut. He was still reeling from it.

Could he ask someone—who was he kidding?—could he ask Lily—to stick with him through it? He didn't know how he would be in a week's, two weeks', two months' time, let alone a lifetime. Would it be fair to tie her down to such uncertainty?

'You may kiss the bride.'

Raoul looked at his hands where they were gripping the arms of his chair like claws. He was happy for Rafe. Of course he was. Rafe was a good brother. A great brother. He deserved to be happy after all he had done for Raoul and Remy. He had kept them together; sacrificed his own interests and at times his safety to keep them as a family.

But it was just so damned hard to be here like...*like this*.

He dragged his gaze towards the bride and groom. Rafe was grinning as if he had just won the lottery. Poppy was smiling with such love on her face it made Raoul feel sick with envy.

He wanted to be loved like that.

Did Lily love him like that?

Could he risk finding out?

The congregation erupted with spontaneous applause as the bride and groom walked back down the aisle as husband and wife.

Raoul felt every eye on him as he wheeled down after them as part of the official bridal procession. Cameras flashed, the frenzied click of shutters sounding like a round of artillery gunfire. His image would be plastered over every paper in the country and all over Europe to-

morrow. His insides churned at the thought. What had
he been thinking, coming here? Remy could have done
just as good a job—better, actually. At least he'd been
able to stand upright.

He caught Lily's eye as he came past her pew. She
was biting her lower lip, her gaze concerned. Troubled.
Uncertain.

He should never have crossed the boundary he'd
crossed with her, but he hadn't been able to help himself. He had been spellbound by her feistiness, the way
she stood up to him in spite of her initial reluctance to
deal with him.

He forced himself to look away. He would speak to
her later. When they were alone. He would ask her if she
could love him like this.

If she *did* love him like this.

He *had* to know.

'I've been absolutely *dying* to meet you.' Poppy gave Lily
a big, squishy hug. 'Rafe's been telling me how wonderful you've been for Raoul.'

'I don't know about that.' Lily felt her cheeks heating.

'He's doing really well,' Poppy said. 'I can't tell you
how much it means to both of us to have him here. We
thought he wouldn't come. He was so stubborn about
it initially.'

'He can be pretty determined when he makes up his
mind about something.'

Poppy gave her a conspiratorial look. 'It's a Caffarelli
trait. Believe me; I know that first-hand. Have you met
Vittorio, the grandfather?'

'No, I saw him at the ceremony, but not to speak to.'

'Don't go near him. He's out for blood. I can handle

most people, but he scares the living daylights out of me.' She gave a little shudder and then smiled widely as Rafe came over. 'Hello, darling.'

Rafe planted a kiss to her mouth. 'Hello, *ma chérie*. Is it time to leave? Please tell me it is. My face is aching from smiling so much.'

Poppy grinned as she linked her arm through one of his. 'We're not going anywhere until we've done the bridal waltz. I think I can hear the band warming up.' She turned and smiled at Lily. 'Will you excuse us? I think that's our cue.'

Raoul was on to his third glass of wine when the bridal waltz started. He wasn't interested in getting drunk or even tipsy. He wasn't trying to mask his pain. He just wanted to block out the smiling faces.

Everyone was so damned happy.

Rafe and Poppy took the floor. They moved together like poetry in motion. Rafe looked so strong and in control, Poppy so feminine and dainty. Their footwork was in perfect tune. No toes were being crushed. No legs were suddenly collapsing.

His stomach clenched.

He would never be able to do the bridal waltz. It was like a boulder hitting him out of nowhere. It crashed against his chest, almost making him double over in pain.

He hadn't been able to be a proper best man. How could he ever be a proper groom?

Raoul was wheeling his chair further away from the dance floor when he overheard two women talking behind one of the pillars. He stopped pushing and went very still, every muscle in his body tensing. Even his scalp pulled tight, making every hair stand up on end.

'Is that slim dark-haired girl Raoul Caffarelli's new mistress?'

'Quite a change from the last one.'

'I heard she's his physical therapist,' the first woman said. 'He must be more like his grandfather than the other two boys, eh?'

Raoul felt his stomach roil. He could not think of anything worse than being compared and likened to his grandfather.

The other woman made a sound of cynical assent. 'Sleeping with the help. Such a Vittorio thing to do. Mind you, that girl is obviously after Raoul for his money. I mean, he's good-looking and all that, but would you really want to spend the rest of your married life pushing him around in a chair?'

Raoul's stomach pitched again and a sickly sweat broke out over his brow.

'It would depend on whether he could still get it up.'

The two women shared a ribald cackle that grated on Raoul's nerves until he thought he would be physically sick.

'For that amount of money I wouldn't care if he *couldn't* get it up. Think of the other compensations: unlimited money to burn, jewellery, designer clothes to wear and luxury holidays to indulge in, not to mention that amazing château in France. What a life.'

'Yes, indeed,' the other woman said. 'No wonder she's got her claws in him so quickly. But how would he know if she loved him or not? Mind you, he probably doesn't care. Better to be with someone than no one when you're disabled. Got to feel sorry for him, though. I always thought he was the nicer of the three, didn't you?'

Raoul turned away in disgust. It was already happening. People were discussing him, talking about him, gossiping, conjecturing about him. It would be a thousand times worse once the press released all those photos of him from the ceremony.

The tragic invalid; the impotent, invalid brother.

He clenched his jaw so hard he thought his teeth would crack. How could his life have come to this?

People mocking him, feeling sorry for him, *pitying* him.

Remy swaggered over with a glass of whiskey in his hand. 'You're not out there to see their first dance. What's wrong with you?'

Raoul gave him a look that would have felled a three-hundred-year-old tree. 'You're not out there burning up the floor, either. No one taken your eye?'

'One of the bridesmaids is cute. I think her name is Chloe, but Poppy has warned her about me. I'm not making any inroads.'

'I feel your pain.'

Remy grinned. 'What's going on with you and your therapist?'

'She's *not* my therapist.'

Remy reared back as if Raoul had suddenly lunged at him with a sword. 'Whoa there, bro. Was that a raw nerve or what?'

'She's going back to London the day after tomorrow.'

'Why?'

'Because her time is up.'

Remy frowned. 'But she's helped you. You've done better with her than anyone else. You spent weeks in rehab and got nowhere. Four weeks with her and you're almost back on your feet. Why would you quit now?'

Raoul set his mouth. 'I'm not back on my feet.' *Half a minute standing without support is not back on my feet.* 'I might *never* get back on my feet.'

'You don't know that. You can't predict how you'll be. You know what the doctors said—it's a waiting game. It could take weeks or months or even years.'

'That's the whole point. I'm not prepared to wait.'

'So you're just going to send her away?'

'She's got nothing to offer me.'

'That's not what Dominique and Etienne say.'

Raoul narrowed his eyes to angry slits. 'Please don't tell me you've been gossiping about me with the domestic staff.' *Was anyone not gossiping about him?*

'They're not just domestic staff, they're like family to you. They care about you.'

'They're not paid to care about me.'

'Neither is Lily Archer, but she cares. She cares a lot.'

'What would you know?' Raoul said. 'You haven't even met her, or at least only in passing.'

'No, but I've spoken to everyone that has. She's like Poppy—warm, sweet and generous. I can't believe you're such a fool to walk away from someone like that.'

'Aren't you forgetting something?' Raoul gave his younger brother a cutting look. 'I can't walk away from her. I can't *walk* away from anyone.'

Remy put his whiskey glass down with a clunk. 'You're going to break her heart. Think very carefully before you do that.'

Raoul barked out a cynical laugh. 'I cannot believe you are preaching to me about breaking someone's heart. Have you taken a look at yourself lately? You haven't been with a woman more than a week in I don't know how long. That's fifty-two hearts you're breaking per year, right?'

Remy glowered at him. 'We're not talking about me here, we're talking about you.'

'I know what I'm doing.'

'We all think we know what we're doing...'

Raoul studied his younger brother's expression for a moment. 'Is everything all right with you?'

'Sure.' Remy gave him an overly bright smile. 'Everything's just fine.'

'Rafe told me you're dealing with Henri Marchand.'

'I've got it covered.'

'Sure?'

'Sure.'

Raoul wasn't so sure. There was something about Remy's expression that alerted him to an undercurrent of worry. Henri Marchand was a sly man, ruthless and conniving. He would sell his grandmother to make a buck. The only near relative he had was his daughter, Angelique, and God only knew what the price was on *her* head. He only hoped Remy wasn't the one who had to pay it. 'If ever you need an ear...'

Remy gave him a high five. 'I've got to get on the move. People to see. Deals to wheel.'

'What? You're not staying for the toss of the bouquet?

Remy gave a visible shudder. 'Not my turn.' He landed a playful punch on Raoul's shoulder. 'You're next in line. *Ciao.*'

When Lily came back to the reception after freshening up in the ladies' room the crowd was jostling for the bridal bouquet toss. She stayed well back in the room, pretending a disinterest that was at odds with everything inside her. She would have loved to be up there pushing and shoving in the mad grab for the bouquet. It was such a high-spirited, girly thing to do.

But she watched from the sidelines, feeling disjointed, displaced, lonely.

'I've got it!'

'No, it's mine!'

'Get out of my way, you fat cow, it's mine.'

Lily moved aside as a wall of women surged towards her. She put up her hands to shield her face and suddenly found herself holding a bunch of flowers. Not just any bunch of flowers, either.

'Oh...'

Every single female eye in the room was on her. There was a massive round of applause and loud cheering.

'This is not meant for me.' Lily thrust the bouquet at the nearest pair of grasping hands. 'Excuse me...'

Raoul intercepted her as she left the reception room. His expression was dark and brooding, just like the first time she'd met him. His eyes were hard, his mouth was tight and his jaw was clenched. 'Did you do that on purpose?'

Lily felt a nervous flutter pass through her stomach. 'Pardon?'

'The bridal bouquet.' His gaze was bitter. 'A not-so-subtle hint to get me to come to the party, so to speak.'

'Party?' She looked at him blankly. 'What are you talking about?'

His mouth was so thin it looked almost cruel. 'You thought by catching that bouquet it would prompt me to ask you to stay with me, especially with the whole crowd watching and cheering.'

Lily opened and closed her mouth. *'What?'*

'It won't work, Lily.' His tone was hard, brittle, angry. 'I'm not asking you to stay with me. I'm asking you—no, strike that, I'm *telling* you—to leave.'

She could barely speak for the pain his words were causing. She hadn't been expecting him to ask her to stay but neither had she thought he would accuse her of such appallingly manipulative behaviour. Didn't he know her at all?

'You want me to leave, what, *now*?'

His expression was as cold and as hard as marble. 'It would seem rather stupid to fly back to France for forty-eight hours. Your contract with me is over. Consider your work with me done.'

Lily swallowed a painful lump in her throat. But her pride made it terribly important not to show how devastated she was by his heartless dismissal. Surely he could have done it differently? Given her some hope. Left things open-ended.

But no, he had cut her loose.

Cancelled her.

Finished with her.

'Right… Well, then, I guess this is goodbye.'

'Yes.' His answer was clipped. Decisive. Final.

Lily gave him one last smile, her bravest, unaffected, 'my heart isn't breaking into a thousand pieces' smile. 'I think you're a really lovely person, Raoul. I hope you get better. But, even if you don't, I want you to know that there are lots of really decent and genuine women out there who would be happy with you just the way you are.'

Something moved in his eyes. A muscle ticked in his cheek. She held her breath, wondering if he was going to change his mind.

The silence stretched…

But then an impenetrable mask came back down over his features. 'Goodbye, Lily.' And then he was gone.

CHAPTER THIRTEEN

'HAVE YOU HEARD how the honeymooners are doing?' Dominique asked as she poured Raoul's coffee two weeks later.

'They got back from Barbados yesterday.'

There was a little silence.

'Have you heard from Mademoiselle Archer?'

He clenched his teeth. 'No. Why should I? I'm just another client. Our time is over. She did all she could for me and it wasn't enough.'

Dominique pursed her lips in thought. 'Love is a funny thing. It can smack you in the face or it can slowly sneak up on you. But what you should never do is walk away from it. You might not get another chance.'

Raoul gave her a sour look. 'Is this a veiled way of hastening your retirement? I thought you wanted to work until you were sixty.'

'You love her. I know you do. I'm a Frenchwoman; I know about these things.'

'You're my housekeeper, not my life coach. I do not pay you to comment on my private life.'

'Mademoiselle Archer doesn't see the chair when she sees you. She just sees you, just like you see her without her scars.'

Raoul felt a lump come up in his throat. He'd been fighting this wretched loneliness for days. The château was oppressive without Lily here. The days were too long, the nights even more so. But how could he ask her to be with him? She would be signing up for a lifetime of caring.

That's what love is all about. Caring. Commitment.

Seeing Lily catching that bouquet at Rafe and Poppy's wedding had made him panic. He had done what he always did when he felt cornered—he had pushed back. Hard. Cruelly.

He had felt so trapped with everyone cheering and nudging each other. He'd felt claustrophobic, pressured, hemmed in at how everyone seemed to be waiting for him to come forward to claim Lily. He didn't want to be some sort of circus pony. He wanted time to think about what he would be asking her to do.

He wanted her.

He wanted it all: the caring and the commitment, the hope of children.

He wanted Lily so much it was an ache in his bones but he felt like he was going to ruin her life if he asked her to marry him.

What if she finds someone else?

His gut churned at the thought of someone else making love to her. Someone too rough and selfish, someone who wasn't sensitive and understanding about her scars. They would destroy her confidence, her self-esteem. She would go back to being that shy, prickly girl who hid behind layers of unflattering clothes.

You love her.

Of course he loved her. He had fallen in love with her the first time he had kissed her. Something had shifted inside him. And he couldn't shift it back. Making love with her had settled it once and for all.

He loved her and was always going to, chair or no chair.

Was it too late to ask her? Would she forgive him for pushing her away so publicly and so painfully? Everyone had been watching their interaction. He couldn't have chosen a worse place to bring things to an end. Was that why she had kept her features so stoic? So controlled? Had he broken her heart as Remy had warned?

Was it too late to undo that damage?

He looked up at his housekeeper. 'I'm going to London for a few days.'

Dominique beamed. 'I've already packed for you.'

He tried to frown at her but he couldn't quite pull it off. 'You did *what*?'

'I did it two weeks ago. I knew you would come to your senses. You're a good man. The *only* man for Lily. She won't be happy with anyone else and neither will you.'

Lily was filing paperwork when Valerie came into her office. 'You should've left an hour ago. You don't have to work overtime every day. You'll burn out.'

'I'm happy working.' Lily closed the drawer. *It distracts me. It's not like I've got anything better to do except sit at home and cry bucket loads of tears.*

'Has he called?'

Lily stiffened. 'Has who called?'

'You know who.'

She let out a rattling sigh. 'No. He won't. He's too stubborn. Once he makes up his mind, that's it. Game over.'

Valerie gave her a thoughtful look. 'He's been good for you. I've seen the change, Lily. Your clothes, your hair, that little touch of make-up. You look good.'

If only I felt good.

'Thanks.' Lily gave her a brief smile.

'Well, I'm off home.' Valerie gave a tired yawn. 'Thank God it's Friday. It's been a long week.'

It's been a lifetime.

Lily walked home even though the first chill of autumn had sharpened the air. It was another way to pass the time. It was an hour each way but she didn't mind the exercise. It was soothing to put one foot in front of the other and let her mind drift. She thought of Raoul even though she always made a promise to herself when she set off that she wouldn't. It was like a default setting inside her head. Her thoughts kept going back to him no matter how many distractions she put in the way.

She had even started imagining she saw him. Only two days ago she had seen a dark-haired man in a wheelchair at Piccadilly Circus. She'd blinked, her heart slamming against her ribcage, but when she had got closer she'd realised it was someone else.

Was that how her life was going to be now? Always wishing, hoping he would magically appear?

'Lily.'

Now she was hearing his voice. Maybe she really was nuts. Crazy.

Crazy in love.

'Lily. Wait.'

She spun around to see Raoul coming towards her. Her heart gave a lurch. She blinked. No, it was him. She wasn't dreaming. He was in his chair but he had a pair of crutches balanced along one side.

'Raoul...' Her voice was little more than a breath of sound.

He looked gorgeous, tired but gorgeous. He'd had his hair cut for the wedding but right now it looked like he hadn't combed it with anything but his fingers.

'I guess I should be on a white horse or something.' He gave her a lopsided smile. 'That's how it always happens in the fairytales, isn't it? I don't think I've read any with a guy showing up in a wheelchair, have you?'

Lily felt a bubble of hope swell in her chest. 'No, but that's not to say it couldn't happen. It's a fairytale, after all. Anything could happen.'

His gaze drank her in. There was a sudden brightness in his eyes and she almost forgot to breathe. 'Will you forgive me for telling you to leave the way I did?'

'You're apologising?'

His mouth tilted. 'I guess I am. How about that?'

'I forgive you.'

He let out a breath as if he'd been holding it in for ever. 'I was so wrong to react like that. It's a bad habit I have. I've been doing it since I was a kid. Pushing people away, hurting people before I get hurt. It's pathetic. It has to stop.'

'I've done it, too,' Lily said softly.

'I panicked at the wedding. I saw all those people staring at us. At *me*. I overheard two women earlier talking about us. It was awful. I couldn't get it out of my head. I couldn't bear the thought of people thinking you were with me out of pity.' He let out another breath. 'When I saw you holding that bouquet I shut down. It was like a reflex.'

'I didn't do it on purpose,' she said. 'I was trying to avoid it but it practically hit me in the face.'

Raoul smiled. 'Like love, *oui*? I have it on good authority that it can either sneak up on you or smack you in the face. I think it's been a bit of both.'

That bubble of hope in Lily's chest was growing by the second. 'What are you saying?'

'I love you,' he said. 'I've never said that to anyone other than my parents.'

She felt her own eyes fill with tears. She dropped to her knees in front of him and, wrapping her arms around him, buried her head against his chest. 'I love you, too.'

Raoul stroked her silky head as it lay pressed against his heart. 'I'm the one who is supposed to be kneeling in front of you. We're really murdering this fairytale thing, aren't we?'

Lily lifted her head to look at him. 'I can't believe you're here. I keep thinking I'm going to wake up and discover it's all been a dream.'

He stroked a finger down her cheek. 'You are my dream, *ma petite*. My dream come true. I know I'm not ideal husband material. I'm not going to be great at putting the garbage out or changing light bulbs. But, what the hell, I can pay people to do that. So will you marry me?'

Lily smiled through her tears. 'Yes.' She threw her arms around him again and hugged him tightly. 'Yes. Yes. *Yes.*'

Raoul lifted her chin up so he could see her face, her beautiful, loving face. 'You are the best thing that ever happened to me. I've hated every minute of being in this chair but if I hadn't been in it I would never have met you. I can't even imagine how awful my life would have been without you in it. I was physically able but emotionally crippled. You've made me see how important it is to be whole emotionally.' He wiped at his eyes with the back of one of his hands. 'Look, I'm even able to cry now.'

Lily tenderly blotted the pathway of his tears with a series of kisses. 'I love you. I love you. I love you.'

He captured her face in his hands and looked deep into her shining eyes. 'I can't carry you over the threshold, but do you think you could perch on my lap instead?'

Lily got up from the footpath and sat on his lap, winding her arms around his neck. 'Are we going to ride off into the sunset now?'

'You bet we are.' He grinned at her. 'Hold on, *ma chérie*. You're in for one hell of a ride.'

* * * * *

Mills & Boon® Hardback
October 2013

ROMANCE

The Greek's Marriage Bargain	Sharon Kendrick
An Enticing Debt to Pay	Annie West
The Playboy of Puerto Banús	Carol Marinelli
Marriage Made of Secrets	Maya Blake
Never Underestimate a Caffarelli	Melanie Milburne
The Divorce Party	Jennifer Hayward
A Hint of Scandal	Tara Pammi
A Façade to Shatter	Lynn Raye Harris
Whose Bed Is It Anyway?	Natalie Anderson
Last Groom Standing	Kimberly Lang
Single Dad's Christmas Miracle	Susan Meier
Snowbound with the Soldier	Jennifer Faye
The Redemption of Rico D'Angelo	Michelle Douglas
The Christmas Baby Surprise	Shirley Jump
Backstage with Her Ex	Louisa George
Blame It on the Champagne	Nina Harrington
Christmas Magic in Heatherdale	Abigail Gordon
The Motherhood Mix-Up	Jennifer Taylor

MEDICAL

Gold Coast Angels: A Doctor's Redemption	Marion Lennox
Gold Coast Angels: Two Tiny Heartbeats	Fiona McArthur
The Secret Between Them	Lucy Clark
Craving Her Rough Diamond Doc	Amalie Berlin

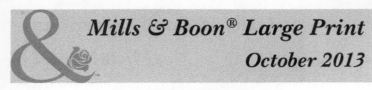

Mills & Boon® Large Print

October 2013

ROMANCE

The Sheikh's Prize	Lynne Graham
Forgiven but not Forgotten?	Abby Green
His Final Bargain	Melanie Milburne
A Throne for the Taking	Kate Walker
Diamond in the Desert	Susan Stephens
A Greek Escape	Elizabeth Power
Princess in the Iron Mask	Victoria Parker
The Man Behind the Pinstripes	Melissa McClone
Falling for the Rebel Falcon	Lucy Gordon
Too Close for Comfort	Heidi Rice
The First Crush Is the Deepest	Nina Harrington

HISTORICAL

Reforming the Viscount	Annie Burrows
A Reputation for Notoriety	Diane Gaston
The Substitute Countess	Lyn Stone
The Sword Dancer	Jeannie Lin
His Lady of Castlemora	Joanna Fulford

MEDICAL

NYC Angels: Unmasking Dr Serious	Laura Iding
NYC Angels: The Wallflower's Secret	Susan Carlisle
Cinderella of Harley Street	Anne Fraser
You, Me and a Family	Sue MacKay
Their Most Forbidden Fling	Melanie Milburne
The Last Doctor She Should Ever Date	Louisa George

Mills & Boon® Hardback
November 2013

ROMANCE

Million Dollar Christmas Proposal	Lucy Monroe
A Dangerous Solace	Lucy Ellis
The Consequences of That Night	Jennie Lucas
Secrets of a Powerful Man	Chantelle Shaw
Never Gamble with a Caffarelli	Melanie Milburne
Visconti's Forgotten Heir	Elizabeth Power
A Touch of Temptation	Tara Pammi
A Scandal in the Headlines	Caitlin Crews
What the Bride Didn't Know	Kelly Hunter
Mistletoe Not Required	Anne Oliver
Proposal at the Lazy S Ranch	Patricia Thayer
A Little Bit of Holiday Magic	Melissa McClone
A Cadence Creek Christmas	Donna Alward
Marry Me under the Mistletoe	Rebecca Winters
His Until Midnight	Nikki Logan
The One She Was Warned About	Shoma Narayanan
Her Firefighter Under the Mistletoe	Scarlet Wilson
Christmas Eve Delivery	Connie Cox

MEDICAL

Gold Coast Angels: Bundle of Trouble	Fiona Lowe
Gold Coast Angels: How to Resist Temptation	Amy Andrews
Snowbound with Dr Delectable	Susan Carlisle
Her Real Family Christmas	Kate Hardy

Mills & Boon® Large Print
November 2013

ROMANCE

His Most Exquisite Conquest	Emma Darcy
One Night Heir	Lucy Monroe
His Brand of Passion	Kate Hewitt
The Return of Her Past	Lindsay Armstrong
The Couple who Fooled the World	Maisey Yates
Proof of Their Sin	Dani Collins
In Petrakis's Power	Maggie Cox
A Cowboy To Come Home To	Donna Alward
How to Melt a Frozen Heart	Cara Colter
The Cattleman's Ready-Made Family	Michelle Douglas
What the Paparazzi Didn't See	Nicola Marsh

HISTORICAL

Mistress to the Marquis	Margaret McPhee
A Lady Risks All	Bronwyn Scott
Her Highland Protector	Ann Lethbridge
Lady Isobel's Champion	Carol Townend
No Role for a Gentleman	Gail Whitiker

MEDICAL

NYC Angels: Flirting with Danger	Tina Beckett
NYC Angels: Tempting Nurse Scarlet	Wendy S. Marcus
One Life Changing Moment	Lucy Clark
P.S. You're a Daddy!	Dianne Drake
Return of the Rebel Doctor	Joanna Neil
One Baby Step at a Time	Meredith Webber